REDEMPTION

US MARSHAL THRILLER SERIES

JODI BURNETT

SDG PUBLISHING

For the officers who were part of a US Marshals Fugitive Task Force who lost their lives in Charlotte, North Carolina during the writing of this book. Thank you for giving your lives to keep people safe. I honor you.

US Deputy Marshal Thomas M. "Tommy" Weeks Jr.
Officer Alden Elliot
Officer Joshua Eyers
Officer Samuel Poloche
"Today we lost some heroes who were out simply trying to keep our community safe." ~ Charlotte-Mecklenburg Police Chief Johnny Jennings

REDEMPTION

US MARSHAL THRILLER SERIES

JODI BURNETT

1

Deputy US Marshal Dirk Sterling was the first to arrive at the office. This was unusual for him, but he was obsessed with hunting down Beaux Crandall. Dirk spent his initial hour in the office poring over all the information he could find regarding Beaux Crandall's escape from his FBI escort and the prison guards on their way to the Super Max facility in Florence, Colorado. There had been no sign of him since, and every day the unresolved investigation ate away at Dirk's insides. He'd finally arrested the scumbag, and the court convicted Crandall of a handful of heinous crimes including murder, human trafficking, child pornography and prostitution, along with drug and arms dealing. The prosecutor also charged him with skipping out on his bail in Louisiana. The judge sentenced Crandall to life in a maximum-security facility, but somehow, on his way to the prison, he got away. He escaped. There had to have been someone helping him on the inside, and Dirk took it personally. The truth was, he wasn't assigned to track

Crandall. Technically, it was an FBI issue because Beaux had been in their custody. But Dirk couldn't leave it alone.

Footsteps approaching the office clattered in the hallway, so he minimized the screen covering Crandall and opened another tab with the case he was supposed to be working on. He went through the police report about an armored truck driver who was killed outside a grocery store in Denver. Police suspected a man named Simeon Gryms of shooting the security officer who left behind a wife and three small children. Gryms's partner in the attempted robbery had also been shot and was now in stable condition under armed guard in the medical jail located in the basement of Denver Health Medical Center. It sounded like he was gushing information to gain some kind of plea deal.

"Good morning, handsome." Chief Deputy Marshal Emory Gray—Dirk's boss and girlfriend—entered the office. She slid her hands over his shoulders and bent to kiss his cheek. She wore her long, blonde hair loose, and it swept over their faces like a curtain and fanned her spicy perfume into his nose. The only reason she openly displayed her affection was because they were the only two in the workplace. She was all business otherwise. "What are you working on?"

He squeezed one of her hands and smiled up at her from his chair. "I'm reading up on the case you assigned me to. Simeon Gryms." He opened another tab behind the police report that displayed Gryms's driver's license photo and basic physical description. "The guy is a total conman. From what I can tell, he's been traveling around the western states duping lonely women into giving him money. A lot of money. His attempt to rob an armored car is an extreme departure from his regular MO. He has no previous record of crime or violence."

"And now he's a murderer."

"A murderer flying under the radar. There have been a couple of reported sightings, but none that have panned out following the armored truck incident. He's grown his hair out and bleached it since he last had his driver's license photo taken."

"Did he get away with any of the money?"

"Yes. He snagged two bags filled with cash to the tune of approximately one-hundred thousand dollars."

"That'll go far in keeping him hidden for a while. Any signs that he's tried to leave the country?"

"No. But that doesn't mean he didn't. Our borders are so porous these days, they're practically like a colander."

Teresa Mendez, the team's Admin's voice, echoed in the hall. She was on the phone as she approached, and Emory moved away from Dirk, walking toward her personal office. Teresa dropped her purse and tote on her desk and rolled her eyes at Dirk, implying irritation with whomever she was talking to.

"I understand that, but the doctor said Tomas was no longer contagious. He feels good, and I have a job I need to be at. I can't afford to miss work." Teresa gripped the back of her chair with her free hand and listened. "Fine. Let me see what I can do. I'll get there as soon as I can." She tossed her phone onto the pile of bags covering her desktop.

"Everything okay?" Dirk swiveled his seat around to face her.

Teresa raked her fingers through her long, black hair and wrenched it into a ponytail that she secured with an elastic band she had on her wrist. "That was Tomas's school. He came home on Friday afternoon with strep throat. I took him to the clinic right away when I picked him up, and they gave him an antibiotic. The doctor told me he would no longer be contagious after twenty-four hours. It's been over forty-eight, but the principal is refusing to let him come back so soon. They want report of a negative test. I can't afford all these tests just to make them feel good."

Emory stepped out of her office. "Teresa, it's okay. We're only doing research today. Nothing's on fire. You can work remotely this afternoon if that helps."

Teresa sighed. "Thanks, boss. I just don't want you thinking I can't do my job 'cuz I've got a kid."

"You always do your job." Emory had removed the hunter-green pantsuit blazer she was wearing and the sleeveless fuchsia blouse she had on underneath deepened the hue of her bright emerald eyes. "That's never a question. Go get Tomas, and if he's feeling up to it, do something fun. I'll let you know if we need you for anything this afternoon."

Teresa studied Emory as if she didn't quite believe she was getting a day-pass. "I can use my PTO."

"Absolutely not. And before you think I'm being nice, think again. I expect you to answer your phone if I call, so it's not a day off."

Dirk loved this side of Emory. She was naturally

sweet and thoughtful, but she always tried to hide her kindness behind a tough-guy demeanor. Her act was never convincing, but it was charming.

Teresa gave Emory a terse smile and nod, grabbed her bags, and left the way she came. Henry Flannigan, or Hank, as Dirk liked to call his younger partner, got to the office as Teresa walked out. He stood sideways to let her through the door and shot a look at Dirk. "Something I said?"

Dirk explained the situation and quipped, "So you'll actually have to do some of your own work today."

"Just mine? Not yours too? Sounds like a simple day, then." Hank chuckled and headed to the breakroom. "Coffee?"

"Yeah, thanks. I sent you an email with the research I've done so far on that Gryms guy."

Hank set a steaming mug next to Dirk's computer and swiped his longish blond bangs to the side. The outside phone line rang, and Emory answered it from her office. A minute later, she strode to Dirk's desk, pushed his coffee aside to give herself room to sit, and clicked a button on his office phone, which opened the call to the speaker.

"Okay, Ms. Linden. You are now on speakerphone. Will you please repeat what you told me so my colleagues can hear too?"

A woman's voice floated from the device. "Yes, as I said, my name is Missy Linden and I'm calling because I was watching the news, and they were reporting on a robbery in Denver. They showed the two suspects' pictures, and I can't tell you how shocked I was when I recognized one of them."

Dirk's blood percolated. "Which one?"

"Well, the name under the photo was Simeon something, but I know the man as Don Walton."

Sitting forward, Dirk asked, "Simeon Gryms? You are acquainted with him?" He shared an excited glance with Emory and Hank and jotted the name Don Walton on a notepad.

"Yes, I know him. He's changed his hair, and he looks like a surfer now, but I know it's him. Last time I saw Don, his hair was brown, and he kept it trimmed. But I still recognized him. I was so upset when the news plastered his face on the TV. That man lived in my home. I trusted him!"

Emory spoke in a soothing tone. "We're so glad you called, Ms. Linden. Where is it you live?"

"In Brentwood, California. Oh, my God. I can't believe I let him... Well, I let him into my whole life. Is he dangerous? Should I be scared?"

"We think he is in hiding. I'd like to send a couple of my deputies out to speak with you. They can be in California by early afternoon. Are you available?"

Dirk glanced at Hank. Sudden travel never went well on the kid's home front. His wife, Amy, was not one to have grace for her husband's surprise absences, and if they were flying to LA in a couple of hours, they wouldn't be back until the following day.

Emory lifted the receiver and took the rest of the call personally. She wrote details on Dirk's pad.

She hung up and tore the sheet of paper off the pad,

handing it to Dirk. "Since Teresa's not here, I'll handle your travel arrangements."

"You're so sure this lady is the real deal?"

"Yes. She described Gryms's likeness on his license, and the police haven't shared it publicly yet. Go talk to her. She says he lived with her for a time. It's likely she knows more than she realizes."

2

Hank stared at the luxurious mansions passing by in Brentwood as Dirk navigated the streets according to the Google Maps app. "Holy crap. It's hard to believe these palaces are single-family homes. Amy was angry because I was going to California. She'd be furious if she knew I got to see all these homes of the rich and famous."

"Single—exceedingly *wealthy*—family homes," Dirk said as he turned onto the street where Ms. Linden's house was located. "And it's not like we're on a vacation or headed to the beach. We're hunting a fugitive."

"Yeah, I doubt those details will matter to Amy."

They stopped outside a gated drive, and Dirk pressed a button on a freestanding intercom. "Hello? Please state your business." A male voice tinged with a tinny echo called out to them.

"Deputy US Marshals Sterling and Flannigan, to see Ms. Linden."

"One moment, please." The box clicked, and seconds

later the heavy gate before them slid away, allowing them to enter.

They drove up a cement drive that had to be a quarter of a mile long and wound through a verdant lawn dotted with palm trees. The road opened to a tiled square lot edged with a two-foot tall, immaculately trimmed privet hedge. Hank's mouth flopped open as he stared at the house before them. Dirk parked next to a white Bentley, and they stepped out of their rental. Hank's gaze took in two other high-dollar cars lined on the other side. A silver Aston Martin Vantage, and a black Mercedes G-Wagon.

Ms. Linden's home was a Mediterranean style, multi-storied mansion with stately columns, arched windows, and a terracotta tiled roof. A grand balcony overlooked the lawn, whose sprinkling system was busy saturating the green carpet. The wide front door opened and a man in a white linen suit stepped out onto the broad porch draped in a slight citrusy smelling hot-pink bougainvillea.

"This way, gentlemen. Ms. Linden is awaiting you at the pool."

Hank followed Dirk as they entered the cool interior of the modern-day palace.

The man—did people still have butlers?—closed the door behind them. "Follow me, please."

Hank couldn't keep his eyes from wandering the elegant space within. Large terracotta tiles paved the floor in the open concept design. Antiques that reminded him of Rome filled the rooms, and he supposed the artwork on the walls was original. They wound around the house until their guide finally came to a section of glass floor-to-ceiling windows he opened like an accordion to a patio that spanned the width of the gargantuan home.

Outside, at a table near a long rectangular pool, sat a woman Hank guessed was in her late forties or early fifties. It was hard to tell with the taut permanent expression of mild surprise her obvious plastic surgery left her with. She wore her shoulder-length blonde hair pulled into a ponytail and threaded through the back of a woven sun hat.

"Madame, Deputy Marshals Sterling and Flannigan." The butler, or manservant, or whatever his official title was, lifted a chair out from the table, and indicated they sit.

"Thanks." Before Dirk took the offered seat, he nudged another one out with the toe of his boot for Hank.

"May I get you gentlemen something to drink?"

Ms. Linden waved her hand imperiously. "Gerald, bring the drinks tray and have Gabriela prepare us a snack." She sipped from a sweating martini glass. "I'm sure you boys are hungry after your flight."

The next moments consisted of introductions and refreshments. The "snack" ended up being cold lobster salad on warm buttery croissants, a watercress dish, and decadent flourless brownies that Hank couldn't get enough of. He watched for Dirk's lead, but his partner seemed content to relax after their meal in the luxury of their surroundings and Ms. Linden's superfluous chatter, taking his time to begin the interview.

"Do you live here alone?" Dirk asked their hostess.

"Yes, besides the staff, of course." She blinked thick false eyelashes. "It gets rather lonely."

Sterling was on his second Arnold Palmer when he finally asked, "How did you come to know Simeon Gryms, Ms. Linden?"

She reached across and laid her hand on Dirk's forearm. "Please, call me Missy."

Hank thought the name Missy was more fitting for a younger woman, but then Ms. Linden was once young, he supposed. She was not a natural beauty, but she spared no expense in the effort. Her makeup was flawless and held up to the warmth of the afternoon. A flowing silk caftan covered her ample curves, and she wore a matching scarf around the brim of her hat.

"Missy." Dirk's voice dipped, and he offered the woman his alluring ghost of a smile. Hank wondered if his partner was flirting or merely trying to make Missy feel comfortable.

"And you're Dirk. Is it alright if I call you Dirk? I don't like all the formalities. They make me nervous."

"Yes, I'm Dirk. And my friend here is Hank." He swirled his drink, making the ice tinkle against his glass. "You were about to tell me how you met Simeon Gryms, or Don Walton, as you knew him."

DIRK ALLOWED Missy Linden to leave her hand on his arm. If that's what it took for her to feel like confiding in him, he'd play along. Hank's expression was priceless. The kid had no guile and certainly no poker face. He'd had a few rough knocks in his young life, but they hadn't hardened him. Yet.

Missy began her tale. "We met at happy hour at the Skybar in LA. I was there with some girlfriends. Don was alone, and we invited him to join us. He bought us all rounds of drinks and one thing led to another." She squeezed Dirk's arm as she said this. Hank sent him a hard look and excused himself to go to the bathroom. "Oh, darling. Use the one in the pool house. It's the closest." Missy waved him toward a building that was as big as a proper home.

When Hank left, Missy scooted her chair closer to Dirk. "Anyway, my two friends are married and wanted to get home, but Don invited me to dinner. He was so handsome then. Not like his picture on the TV." She took a break to refill her martini from an iced pitcher. When she turned back to Dirk, her knee rubbed up against his. "We went downstairs to the restaurant. Oh, my God, Dirk." She clutched his arm again. "The food there is to die for. Have you ever been?"

"I haven't had the pleasure." Generally, her type of dramatic retelling drove him crazy. But Dirk knew if he wanted her story, he was going to have to wade through it.

"Well, maybe we should fix that." Missy swayed forward, presenting him with a view of tired cleavage.

When he returned, Hank cleared his throat before taking his seat, and Missy had the grace to sit back in her chair. "What are you fixing?"

Missy giggled, and Dirk figured she was more than a little tipsy after a day of indulging in martinis. "I was saying we should go to dinner at the Skybar tonight. You boys don't have any plans, do you?"

"My plan is to listen to your story." Dirk hoped to refocus the woman.

"Right, well, we had a wonderful evening, and things were clicking between us. When you know—you know. Right?" She sat up and adjusted her silk. "At the end of the evening, Don went to handle the check and realized he'd left his wallet in his hotel room. He was mortified. I felt awful for him."

Hank filled his glass with cucumber and lemon infused water. "What did he do?"

"What could he do? I told him not to worry, that I'd take care of the bill and he could pay on another occasion. I thought I was so clever, setting up a next time. Anyway, he drove me home and one thing led to another... you know?" She gave Dirk a meaningful look, and it took everything in him not to bust out laughing. Missy was beyond obvious. It was sad in a way.

"He stayed that night, and he never left. He lived here for about a month. I never suspected anything. I mean, he wore Armani, for God's sake, and he had a Rolex. His car was a rental because he was in town on business. So, I told him to return it and I leant him my little red Cadillac. He said he had a meeting up in San Fran for a couple of days, so I let him take the Caddy and that was the last time I saw him. Since then, I've noticed some of my jewelry is missing and a small Vermeer painting I kept in one of the guest bedrooms."

Missy pressed the tail of her silk hat scarf against the corner of her dry eyes as if she had tears. "I'm so embarrassed." She dropped the fabric and crunched her brows together. "And I'm angry. You need to catch that scoundrel and put him in jail."

Dirk covered her leathery hand with his. "Did he say what kind of business he had in San Francisco? Or where he was staying?"

"No. I didn't ask him a lot of questions. I was in love—I trusted him. And I didn't want to come across as too needy."

"My wife is in love too, but she asks me tons of questions," Hank added dryly.

Missy glanced at him. "Clearly, I should have been more suspicious. What can I say? But now, I'd like to help you find him."

Dirk scooted his chair back. "We'll need the license plate number of your car. Did you report it stolen?"

"No." Missy looked at her hands now resting in her lap. "I was still hoping he'd return until I saw him on TV."

"Call the police as soon as we leave and report it stolen. That will get the theft on record in the system. If we're lucky, he'll get pulled over for a minor traffic violation, and we'll have him." Dirk stood, and Hank followed suit. "Missy, thank you for lunch and for the information. You're more help than you realize."

He offered his hand, but instead of shaking it, Missy clasped it to pull herself up and then held on to him all the way to the front door, grasping both his palm and elbow. Dirk gently extracted himself from her so they could leave.

"Thanks again, Missy. Have a nice evening." He peeled her fingers from his biceps and stepped away.

With laughter sparking in his eyes, Hank waved rather than offer her his hand. "Thanks for the sandwiches. We'll be in touch."

"Yes," Dirk added. "And don't forget to report your stolen car and any other missing items. Please do that right now. It would be a great help for us. And have a good night."

"I wish you boys would let me take you to dinner. You're not flying back to Montana tonight, are you? We could go to the Skybar, and you could see where I met Don. It would be my treat." Missy tilted her head, her eyes pleading with him.

He felt bad for the woman. She was desperately lonely. But he wasn't about to get caught up in that. "Thanks, but we have another meeting in an hour. This trip is all work, I'm afraid."

Her silky billows seemed to deflate. "Alright. Maybe next time?"

Dirk nodded, and turning, stepped off the porch. Hank chuckled under his breath, but he said nothing until they got inside the car. "I can't wait to hear what the Chief will say when she hears she has some serious competition here in LA."

"And yet, Emory won't hear about Missy's behavior, will she, Hank?"

"Oh, right. What happens in LA stays in LA. No—that's Vegas. I don't think the rule applies here. Sorry, dude."

3

A soft breeze lifted the sparse tufts of hair that remained on the side of Beaux's bald head and rattled the palm fronds overhead. He cast his gaze out at the lapping water on the beach edge before raising his hand to the tiki bartender, who stood nearby, constantly ready to serve. The local man, who had on the blue and gold dashiki uniform worn by all of Beaux's servants, hurried over to take his master's drink order.

"Bring us each another Dawa." Beaux ordered for himself and his guests.

Addicted to the refreshing local cocktail, Beaux watched as the server cut limes into four cubes and dropped them to cut-crystal baccarat glasses. Over the citrus quarters, he sprinkled a spoonful of sugar, and added large dollops of honey since Beaux liked his drinks nectarous. He then muddled the mixture, squishing the lime juice into the sweetness. Traditionally, mixologists crafted the drink using vodka, but his guests preferred gin and Beaux enjoyed his made with cognac. The flavor reminded him of his southern Louisiana roots and paired well with the salty sea breeze.

"So refreshing," Nasir murmured as he sipped his cocktail. The young Saudi prince was dressed in all white, loose-fitting Egyptian cotton, the brightness of which highlighted the dark liquidity of his eyes. His gaze perused the youthful merchandise playing at the water's edge under the watchful eye of their guard.

Tariq, the prince's attendant, or friend—maybe both —Beaux wasn't clear on their relationship, donned similar attire to the prince only in a cream tone. He was more interested in the chemical forms of entertainment offered on the island than the sexual smorgasbord Beaux provided. Tariq's desires were easier to provide and equally addictive.

"See something you like, your Highness?" Beaux's southern drawl smoothed over his words.

"Perhaps. Perhaps." Nasir returned his gaze to Beaux. "But there is time for that later. I want to hear more about how you ended up here, on this island. It must seem like the end of the world to you after living in the US. I imagine you had to leave a fortune behind."

"Well, now. That's a long tale best told over more booze." Beaux nodded to the bartender, who was there to serve them alone. After all, the tiki bar belonged to Beaux, along with the private beach and the entire compound that included his palatial mansion, ten exquisitely appointed bungalows for guests, and a barracks for his chattel. No one came—or left, for that matter—without Crandall's express permission.

Beaux began his story. "I have successfully avoided

incarceration by the law my entire adult life—and it has been an eventful life, let me tell you—until last spring, when unfortunately, US Marshals arrested me. The state of Montana prosecuted me for a few very minor incidences." Sarcasm spiced Beaux's tone.

The men laughed together at the extreme understatement of what they knew were Beaux's salacious crimes—crimes they were on his island to take advantage of and enjoy for a mind-sizzling price.

"Yes." Nazir grinned. "But how did you get away? Weren't you under guard?"

"Of course I was. But I had the smarts," Beaux tapped his head, "to have a plan in place in case such an event ever occurred. When my trial hit the news, that arrangement went into motion. There were three vehicles in the convoy escorting me to what would have been life in prison, but some dear and extremely expensive friends of mine were lying in wait to rescue me. They torched the first car with an incendiary round, fired from a shoulder launcher. Blew the damn thing clear off its tires. It was a beautiful sight. They riddled the second vehicle with bullets from a machine gun, killing everyone inside. The guards in my transport had it easy. When they pulled to a stop and attempted to surrender, they graciously received a simple shot to the back of their heads."

Manic excitement danced in the dark eyes of Beaux's guests as he continued. "Within minutes, I was on my way out of Colorado and was completely out of the country before the story hit the news." Beaux drained his glass. "My favorite thing to imagine is the expression that must have been on US Deputy Marshal Dirk Sterling's face when he heard I got away. I wish I could have seen it. He thought he had stopped me, but in truth, his efforts merely inspired me to think bigger."

Beaux smirked and poured himself a fresh glass of Dawa from an insulated pitcher placed on the counter for refills. He noticed Tariq's fidgeting increased as the afternoon wore on—twitching in his need for a fix. The man's addiction got Beaux thinking. If he could set up an account with the prince, it would mean another consistent flow of income—a drug subscription of sorts. He'd already developed a lucrative route for multiple types of drugs from Pakistan. And, if he provided his wares efficiently, he was certain Nasir would quietly share the information with his friends and family. Business was booming. Soon it would be exploding.

"Tariq, I believe I'm being rude in my neglect. Where are my manners?" Beaux gave the man a slight bow. "Would you care for a line or two of powdered candy with your drink?"

The royal attendant's body was all bones and angles. His eyes protruded over a large, hooked nose that sprouted a thin mustache. Tariq nodded and guffawed a donkey braying sort of laugh. Beaux wondered if the prince kept him around simply to set off his own handsome features and charm. There was nothing else to recommend the man as far as Beaux could see.

In that moment, a sharp dart of grief pierced Beaux's chest. The thought of deep friendship brought back his grief of losing Troy—the only person Beaux had ever trusted. Troy was like a brother to him, the only friend he ever had, and his death sat squarely on Deputy Marshal

Sterling's head. One day Beaux would make Sterling pay. He knocked back his drink, appreciating the light sway he felt, but knowing it would take the rest of the pitcher to help him ease the pain.

Beaux was wealthy beyond scope, but he was lonely, too. Even with all the people he kept on his island, none of them reached his deep, well protected heart in the way his friendship with Troy had.

"Mamadou," Beaux called to the server. "Bring our guests some snow to cool off their afternoon."

Nasir, more interested in Beaux's story than the fun he had paid to enjoy, waved away the cocaine when the bartender offered it to him, allowing Tariq to fill his enormous nostrils with the lines. "Where did you go when you first left the States? And how did you end up here? It doesn't seem like it took you long to set up your lucrative business in this lovely paradise." Nasir gestured to the mansion and the beach beyond with a sweeping hand.

"You are very curious. Why so many questions, my friend? You know, in my profession, too many questions make me nervous."

Nasir scoffed at the veiled threat. The young prince must have truly believed he was above such dangers. "No need to be apprehensive about my curiosity. I am impressed by your adventures. I would love to have such experiences of my own."

"Well, that's why you came here, isn't it? You told our contact that you wanted to try something... new. Why don't we get you started on your various trysts?"

Beaux refilled Nasir's drink and handed him the glass. He slid his arm around the man's shoulders and walked him toward the beach. "Take your choice, your High-ness." Beaux held his hand out, indicating the young women he had stocked and groomed for the prince's purview.

"You received my request? That I desire six fully waxed virgins? I want them to look like—" Nasir couldn't bring himself to finish the sentence.

Beaux smiled. "Like little girls? Of course. We've followed every nuance of your request. But may I suggest, Prince Nasir, instead of asking for women who look like girls, why don't you simply select the age you truly desire? There are no boundaries here on my magic island. We can easily fulfill your every wish and fantasy. No matter how... *creative* it might be."

Nasir's eyes flared, and he swallowed. "Anything?"

"Of course. My dear Prince. You are already able to procure what you asked for when you're at home. So, why come here? I'll tell you why. Because here you can have what you *really* desire. Perhaps things you didn't even know you wanted. I have a video library filled with stimu-lating ideas to inspire you."

Beaux crooked his finger at one of the young women near them. She approached but kept her gaze on the sand at their feet. "Go tell Carlos to bring the children."

Her dark brows stitched together, and for a brief moment, Beaux thought she might refuse him. It would cost her dearly if she did. But after an obvious internal struggle, she hurried up the beach to the barracks-type building where he housed his merchandise.

4

Laurie Dillinger sat before her large desktop computer monitor, clicking through her old graphic design portfolio. It was hard for her to believe she was the one who had created all the engaging images that flashed before her. It seemed so long ago. A year and a half had passed since her husband, Sam, died in an explosion while he was on the job. The pain of missing him was still acute, but the sharp edges that sliced through her heart had softened a little. He had been working down in Wyoming with Caitlyn Reed and her K9 partner, Renegade. The US Marshals sent them there to protect a federal judge who'd received several death threats. Both Sam and the judge died when a bomb exploded in the judge's chambers.

A couple of months ago, Laurie believed she had fallen in love with Dirk Sterling. Dirk and Sam were partners before her husband died. They were also close friends, and Dirk had a wonderful relationship with her young son, Caleb. He was like an uncle to the boy, and it was easy for her to imagine him fitting into their lives, but Dirk didn't share her feelings.

He wanted Emory Grey. Dirk was a good man and doing his best to protect her pride, he let her down gently. He never stopped coming by—even though it had to be uncomfortable for them both after she'd come on to him —to help around the house doing the chores Sam had always done and hanging out with Caleb. Laurie was grateful to have a such a positive male influence in her son's life.

But it was time to pick up her own life and get on with it. She had left her graphic design business when she got pregnant with Caleb and had poured herself into being a mother. Since Sam's death they'd been living on his life insurance and the money the USMS issued for his death in the line of duty. Laurie was finally ready to become the provider for their little family. She had some solid art samples in her folder but wanted to add some fresh, updated examples before she put herself out there.

A thrill zipped through her belly as she let herself dream. But was she crazy to try? Maybe she should get a job in retail. Laurie bit her lower lip. Retail might be safer, but it would never allow her the flexibility she required to raise her young son. A sense of self-doubt had her pushing away from her desk to seek the comfort of a steaming mug of Earl Grey.

She almost missed the phone call when the gurgling noise of water boiling in the kettle drowned her ringtone. "Hello?" She was breathless from running back to her office.

"Laurie?"

"Yes?"

"This is Dave. Dave Aldrich. I'm friends with Emory Grey and Dirk Sterling?"

"Yes, of course, Dave. I remember." How could she forget? He was at Dirk's dinner party, where she had made a complete fool of herself. Thankfully, Dave hadn't seen. Dirk had graciously saved her from public humiliation, but she still remembered everyone who was there—vividly.

Dave broke through her mortifying memory. "We talked about having coffee sometime."

"Yes."

"That's why I'm calling. If you're interested, maybe we could get together sometime this week?"

The weight of her embarrassment lightened. It felt good to have a solid, good-looking man pursuing her. "Sure. Caleb is in preschool on Monday, Wednesday, and Friday." She paused. "But you probably have to work during the day. Daytime might not work for you."

He chuckled. "I can get away for an hour or so. How's tomorrow? Say ten o'clock at the Legal Grounds?"

"That's the place down by the courthouse, right?"

"Yeah, you know it?"

"Sure do. I'll meet you there."

"Great. I'm looking forward to seeing you again."

"Me too." Laurie hung up, and holding her phone to her chest, she bounced around in a tight circle. Her heart raced like a teen who was on her first date. Her nerves popped and jangled.

The kettle whistled, and she returned to the kitchen to toss the tea bag into her mug. Stirring in a spoon of sugar, she mused over the fact she seemed drawn to men with dangerous jobs. First, Sam, who was a deputy marshal, and then Dirk, another deputy who was constantly throwing himself into alarming situations, and now Dave, who was an FBI agent. She shrugged and sipped the hot bitter drink. At least, men like them kept life interesting

THE NEXT MORNING, after changing outfits three times, Laurie drove to downtown Billings and squared the block around the Yellowstone County Court House. She left her car in the parking garage and walked down Third Avenue to the coffee shop where Dave was waiting for her. He stood and waved as she entered the cozy little café. She breathed in the fresh-ground roasted scent of the fancy coffees on their menu.

"Laurie. It's good to see you." He reached for her hand and leaned in to kiss her cheek. "Have a seat and I'll go order. What can I get you?"

"A London Fog, please." Laurie slid off her wrap and sat down when Dave held her chair for her. "Thanks."

She took advantage of the unguarded opportunity to watch him as he waited in line. Dave was around six feet tall, about the same as Sam, but shorter than Dirk. He parted his brown hair neatly on the side and wore it in a practical cut, absent any personal styling methods. His crisp white shirt stood out against his navy-blue suit and matching tie, which Laurie thought was very FBI-ish of him.

Dave turned and caught her looking at him. He

flashed her a handsome smile comprised of even white teeth before he ordered their beverages. Carrying the cups to their table with a plate of scones balanced on his arm, he handed Laurie her tea before he took his seat across from her.

"I'm really glad we could make this happen." Dave sipped his black coffee. "How have you been since I saw you last?"

"Good, thanks. I've been thinking of going back to work."

"Really? What kind of work do you do?"

Suddenly bashful, Laurie glanced around at the artfully decorated coffee shop. People wearing headphones or earbuds and working on their laptops filled the inviting space. Perhaps they were writers or entrepreneurs building their dreams.

"I had my own one-person graphic design company before Caleb was born. I put my business aside so I could focus on being a mom, but now I think it's time to dust it off again. Caleb will be in school full time next year, and I figure I could build my clientele back up over the next several months and then hit it hard in the next year."

"That's impressive. What type of art do you design?"

"Mostly marketing copy. I've done a few book covers and lots of work for civic organizations and small businesses here in Billings."

"Sounds like you already have some solid connections. You'll do great."

Laurie smiled at his encouragement. She had forgotten the uplifting feeling of having the support of someone she admired and was attracted to. "How about you? How's the FBI business going?"

"Nothing very exciting lately, not since Beaux Crandall escaped. I've mostly been riding the desk. It isn't always like the movies."

"Not so different from what my husband Sam and Dirk do... did." She flushed. "You know what I mean."

Dave patted her hand. "I do. And I'm really sorry about what happened to Sam. How is Caleb coping with all of it?" He left his hand resting on the table next to hers, and she had the urge to slip her fingers through his, but she was nervous. Their friendship was too new.

Instead, she helped herself to a scone, breaking off a crumbly corner. "He's doing remarkably well now. It's been over a year. But honestly, I have to give Dirk the credit. He spends a lot of time being the man in Caleb's life. He's a loyal friend."

Something shifted in Dave's eyes that she couldn't pinpoint, but his tone remained kind. "Sam and Dirk were partners, right? He's probably doing all that out of loyalty to your husband."

"Yes. They were very close. The three of them, actually. Sam and Dirk often worked with a deputy out of Wyoming. Have you met Caitlyn Reed? She's a K9 handler for the Marshals. She is the one who gave Bear to Caleb. My son and his dog have been inseparable ever since."

"A tight US Marshal family." Dave lifted his scone and dipped a corner into his coffee.

"Exactly. Is it the same in the FBI?"

"It can be, but I haven't found that to be true at this office."

"I'm sorry. I know for Law Enforcement families the connections are crucial."

"Maybe it's because I don't have a wife and kids of my own."

"Possibly, but don't you have any get-togethers with your coworkers?"

"Not so much."

"Well, since you are friends with everyone in the Billings USMS office, you'll have to come to ours. They still include Caleb and me, which I love."

"I don't know. Emory Grey and I dated for a while and Dirk and I, well... I'm sure you understand."

"I don't think that needs to stand in your way. There was a time when I believed something might happen between me and Dirk, but I was wrong. I misunderstood what I thought were some signals and ended up uber embarrassed, but things are clear now and I still enjoy spending time with the gang."

"Sounds kind of like my situation with Emory."

"Exactly. So, see? You should hang out with us. No one will make you feel weird. We are adults, after all."

Dave smiled but didn't seem convinced. "What are your marshal friends working on these days?"

"I don't know. But Dirk seems obsessed with that Beaux Crandall guy."

"Is he still actively trying to hunt him down?"

"Not officially. Emory sent Hank and him to LA on some other case. They'll be gone until tomorrow."

"LA? So, not Crandall?"

"Not right now. But honestly, I think Dirk will always hunt Crandall until he finally catches him."

"What's the case in LA about, do you know?"

"I don't. We didn't talk long."

"Does Sterling always tell you when he's going out of town?"

"Yeah. He keeps me posted in case Caleb or I need him."

"For what?"

Laurie smiled and sipped her tea. The sweet milky version of the London Fog was a treat. At home she drank her Earl Grey black. "For silly things like when my hot water heater went out, and he had to come over and ignite the pilot light for me. Stuff Sam would have done, I guess."

Dave took her hand in his and rubbed his thumb over her skin, leaving tingles in its wake. "Well, if you ever need anything when he's not around, you can always call me."

"Really?" He was so sweet. Laurie was glad it hadn't worked out between him and Emory.

"Really." He gently squeezed her fingers. "Laurie, would you have dinner with me on Friday night?"

"I'd love to. Thanks." She disciplined her grin into a much more sober one than one that expressed her genuine excitement. "I have to see if I can get a babysitter. But I'm sure it won't be a problem."

"Great. I'll pick you up at your house at 6:30."

5

Emory hadn't slept well. She woke from a nightmare at 3:30 am and couldn't get back to sleep. A recurring dream had haunted her slumber ever since the mission to stop the religious terrorist, Aydin Rahip. It had been her first big case as the new Chief Deputy in Billings. Emory had been in a helicopter with Dirk, Hank, the FBI SAC of the New York City office, Cynthia Toller, the pilot, and a bomb. Toller, who turned out to be a radical Wurunsemu cult member, shot the pilot in the head, and Emory was certain at the time they were all going to die either by explosion or by crashing into Lake Ontario.

In her dream, she was in the helicopter, but when Dirk went to throw the ticking bomb out of the craft and into the lake, he lost his balance and fell with it, tumbling through the sky toward the water. Every time this happened, Emory woke with a jolt, breathless with her heart racing. In the aftermath of the terrifying dreams, she could never calm down enough to get back to sleep.

Once she and Dirk got together, she stopped having the nightmares. Until last night, when she'd had another doozie. Emory ignored the idea that the dream was an omen of some kind. She didn't believe in those kinds of things... did she?

Emory climbed out of bed, took a long hot shower, and dressed for work. She watched the morning news and did the crossword puzzle in the local paper.

Finally, it was a reasonable enough time to go into the office. It was still dark when she let herself into the building. She started a pot of coffee and turned on her computer. It bothered her how much she missed having Dirk at the office and even more so in her bed. This kind of fractured thinking was why she frowned upon inter-office relationships, especially with subordinates. She wasn't one to show favoritism at work. That wasn't the problem. It was that Dirk distracted her. Of course, that was obviously true whether or not he was in the office.

She snickered at herself as she poured her first cup of dark roasted caffeine. Sniffing in the rich scented steam, she settled in to read the daily national crime reports. She cocked her head and narrowed her eyes, carefully attending to the details. Emory glanced at her watch. It was 6:30 am in Billings, which made it 5:30 am in LA. That wasn't too early, was it? Besides, she was hungry to catch Simeon Gryms, and she was about to change Dirk and Hank's plans. They needed to know, and the sooner, the better.

"Good morning, beautiful. Missing me?" Dirk's sleepy voice seeped into her bones.

"Good morning. And yes, as a matter of fact, I am. But

that's not why I'm calling. There has already been a hit on the stolen Cadillac Ms. Linden reported yesterday."

"Where? Was Gryms with the vehicle?"

"No. From what I gather, a woman in Cheyenne called the police over a week ago to report an abandoned car in front of her home. Apparently, her boyfriend left it there and never bothered to return to pick it up. The police hadn't really done anything about it, but when the license plate number for the stolen vehicle was entered into the nationwide system, it flagged them, and they went out to investigate. Sure enough, the car the woman stated as being left at her home is the missing Caddy we're looking for. It wasn't difficult to put the pieces together and figure out that her boyfriend was Simeon Gryms."

"He was in Cheyenne?"

"I suppose he drove it to Denver, committed his crimes, and then used it as a getaway car. He probably drove straight up I-25, the fastest way out of Dodge."

"Well, at least we have the beginning of a trail."

"Yes. And that's why I'm calling. I want you and Henry to fly from LA to Cheyenne today to interview the woman who last saw Gryms. Since she had a relationship with him, she might have an idea where he went. Later this afternoon, there's a military transfer from Warren Air Force Base flying to Billings. You guys can catch a ride home on it afterwards. I'll have Teresa arrange all the travel."

"Okay. Sounds like I might still be home in time for dinner."

"Want me to cook something? You could come to my apartment after you land."

"I'd love to, but Thursdays are my night with Caleb."

"And Laurie." Her tone came across harder than she intended.

"Yes, and Laurie. You're not jealous, are you?" His sultry, teasing tone made her laugh.

"Not really. Not of Laurie, but of your time—maybe."

"My boss is highly demanding." His teasing warmed her. "I'll come by after I see them. How does that sound?"

"Perfect. Call me after you talk to the woman in Wyoming. Her name is Katherine Downy. I'll text you her address and all the pertinent details."

"Good. I'll see you tonight."

"Till then." Emory hung up and was smiling to herself when Teresa came in.

"Morning, Boss."

"You're early."

Teresa opened a drawer in her desk and set her purse inside. "I figure I have work to do to make up for yesterday."

"Not really. Besides, don't you drop Tomas off at school?"

"Sometimes, but on days like today he goes to before-school care."

"He's already in afterschool care, right? Isn't that expensive?"

Teresa stared at her hand resting on the seat back. She nodded and turned on her computer. "But it's what working moms have to do."

"I don't want you to feel you have to make up yesterday's hours, but I admit I'm glad you're here this morning." Emory explained the developments in the case and the need for Dirk and Hank's travel changes. "Will you please make the arrangements?"

"Not a problem. After I grab some coffee."

"I'll get us a cup. I was on my way to the pot myself. When you're done, will you please text Dirk with his itinerary changes and tag me, too?"

Emory hummed as she poured the two cups of dark roast. The Gryms case was hot, and she was determined to find him. He'd defrauded too many unsuspecting women, and she wanted to be the one to shut him down.

Hank woke to someone pounding on his hotel room door. At first, he rolled over, dragging his pillow to cover his head, but the banging did not stop.

"Open up, kid. I brought coffee." His partner's voice broke through his foggy brain.

Hank hated Dirk at that moment. All he wanted was one more hour of sleep. Would that have been too much to ask? Hank stumbled out of bed, unlocked the door, and without waiting for Dirk to enter, he plodded into the bathroom and closed the door behind him.

When he emerged from the john, he glared at Dirk. "What's going on?"

"Chief called me at 5:30 this morning, so stop whining and drink your coffee while it's hot." Dirk handed him a cup. "Cops in Wyoming have already located Missy's stolen Caddy."

"That was fast. Wyoming? Are they sure?"

"Yeah. Cheyenne. Chief wants us to fly there and talk

to the lady who reported it. Don't worry. We'll be home by dinner."

"We'd better be," Hank grumbled, thinking of the hurricane that would tear around his apartment if he wasn't there by six.

He had called Amy before he went to bed last night, but she didn't answer, and his call switched over to voice-mail. He texted her he loved her and hoped she had sweet dreams, but she never returned his message. Hank understood she intended her lack of response as punishment for him doing his job. Again. He tried to give her the benefit of the doubt, considering her fluctuating hormones, but this was just more of the same old game-playing crap. He honestly didn't know what to do to make things better between them.

"Amy's still mad at you?"

Hank shrugged. He would have liked to talk about it, but he figured Dirk probably didn't really want to, and the last thing Hank wanted was to come across like he couldn't handle his own marriage. "Yeah, I guess. She didn't answer my calls last night, so..." He took a burning swig from his coffee cup and grimaced. "I'm gonna shower. I'll be out in five, and then we can go."

"I'll be here."

Under scorching missiles of water, Hank leaned his forehead against the cool tile. It was getting harder to focus on his work through the veil of guilt he had over Amy, but when he was with her, his life was pure hell. Why would he give his career up to feel like that?

But that option—giving up on his marriage—wasn't something he wanted either. What happened to the fun-loving girl he had married? Hank wanted that life back. The life he had before the helicopter accident. Frustrated tears threatened to run with the shower, so he turned the tap to cold and sobered up. What would Dirk think if he knew his partner was in the bathroom crying like a sissy?

The icy stream caused him to suck in his breath and his eyes cleared. He dried off and wrapped a towel around his waist. Dirk was sitting with his legs stretched out on the second bed, watching *Unsolved Mysteries*. He ignored Hank while he dressed and packed his bag.

"Okay. All set. Ready to get out of LA?"

Dirk grunted. "More than you can imagine. When I look out the window, I can't see the horizon through the smog. We're breathing that shit, you know."

"Said the man from the pristine skies of Montana."

"Purest air in the country." Dirk pushed himself off the bed. "Let's grab some breakfast. We have time before our flight."

At the hotel restaurant, Hank ordered a veggie omelet with fresh fruit. One thing he appreciated about California was there were always healthy options on the menu. Dirk chose chicken fried steak smothered with sausage gravy. Obviously, he wasn't concerned about heart health. But to his credit, he only ate half and took the rest in a to-go box. They paid their bill and went to wait for the airport shuttle.

An old man, bent over from age and the ravages of drugs and alcohol, tottered up the sidewalk toward them. His clothes were filthy and worn through at the knees and on one elbow. Clouded but kind eyes regarded them as he approached. He pressed his hands against his belly. "Sir, do you have any change or food to spare?"

The doorman hurried over to rush the man away. "No vagrants or begging allowed on the hotel property. You must leave."

The hunched man sighed and turned to go, but Dirk held up his hand. "Hold on. This man isn't bothering us. He's a friend."

The hotel employee drew his chin back. "But he's a homeless transient. It's my job to keep people like him away from our patrons."

A dark brow rose above Dirk's irritated expression. "If your boss has anything to say, you can tell him to come talk to me. Thank you." Dirk held his hand out to the worn and ragged man. "I'm Dirk."

The old man studied him for a moment before his trembling hand stretched out and took hold of Dirk's. "I'm Lionel. Folks 'round here call me Leo."

"Nice to meet you, Leo. I happen to have some delicious chicken fried steak in this box, just for you."

"Well, that's mighty kind. Thank you, sir."

Dirk handed the man the box, and Hank noticed that as he did, he slipped the old guy a fifty-dollar bill. Tears formed on the man's lower eyelids, and he patted Dirk awkwardly on the arm, too moved to say anything.

"Have a good day, today." Dirk gripped the man's shoulder in farewell.

Hank choked up. Maybe Amy wasn't the only emotional one. He cleared his throat. "The airport shuttle is here."

Dirk lifted his overnight bag and loaded it into the

van. Hank did the same, and they climbed into the back seat.

"Dirk, that was pretty cool—"

Dirk shot a glare in his direction, cutting off his comment. "How much time do we have before our flight?"

6

———

Ayellow bikini-clad Nigerian girl brought Beaux his pot of morning coffee and filled his cup. He sipped the rich brew while drinking in the ocean view from the veranda off his master suite. A soft breeze caressed his skin, and he breathed in its salty freshness. Before he set up shop on the island, he had believed himself to be a mountain-loving man. Now, he couldn't imagine living anywhere but on the beach. Beaux chuckled to himself. He had managed not only to land on his feet after his close brush with the law, but he was moving up in the world.

This early in the morning, the vast stretch of seafront was empty except for his people, who cleaned and graded the sand. They also freshened the linens in the cabanas, popped up umbrella shades, and opened the towel and beach-toy cabinet.

Currently, Beaux had only two guests staying on his island, and briefly he wondered how they were getting along with their fantasy vacation. Prince Nasir himself was a relatively unimportant man compared to some of Beaux's clientele, but if the young royal left happy, he might eventually connect Beaux with one of his uncles who dabbled in smuggling firearms. Sex and drugs—those branches of his business were easy to set up, and the customer list was broad, but guns involved a more specific taste and took far more time and trust. Personal recommendations went a long way, and so Beaux invested in Nasir's dark fantasies coming true.

Beaux padded across white marble tiles to his breakfast table. He should feel utter contentment, but a heavy melancholy lapped at his soul. He and his friend Troy used to have their meetings over the morning meal. Now, it was the loneliest time of the day.

"Chinara!" Beaux called to his servant girl. Beaux selected Chinara, a fourteen-year-old, dark-skinned beauty, for his personal use after his men snatched her off the streets of the port city of Lagos. It took a month or two to break her down, but now she catered to all his whims with no resistance. He liked her, and if she continued to do his bidding without trouble, he'd keep her.

"Yes, Mr. Beaux." The willowy girl kept her gaze cast to the floor.

"Bring me my phone."

She bent her knees and bowed in a show of acquiescence, hurrying off to his rooms in search of the device. Returning quickly, she presented the phone to him, resting on her palms.

"Good." Beaux shifted his robed girth and let his

knees fall open. "Now take off your top and kneel before me."

Chinara's eyes took on the hunted look he so enjoyed seeing, but she did as she was told. She'd learned the hard way that it was much more pleasant to do as he commanded. He watched as she slipped off her bikini top and knelt between his legs. Beaux laughed as he snatched up his phone.

"Before you get started, I have an important call to make." He scrolled through his contacts until he located the number for Maria Cortez. Troy's long-lost mother. His friend had searched for years and finally found her shortly before the feds killed him. Now, in tribute, Beaux was determined to take care of the woman, as he knew Troy would have if he lived.

Both Beaux and Troy grew up in the social services system in Natchitoches Parish, Louisiana. They met in juvenile hall and had become fast friends. The taller of the two boys, Beaux took Troy under his wing and protected him, which is why Troy had been so fiercely loyal. It had always been the two of them against the world—until Dirk Sterling killed him. An act the deputy marshal would eventually pay for dearly.

Two months before his death, Troy had located his birth mother and learned the story of his conception. His mother, Maria Cortez, was in the US illegally and had been working as a live-in housekeeper on the Rainer family estate. Mr. Rainer came to her room one night and raped her. Soon, he was a regular visitor to her bed and before long, she became pregnant with Troy.

Not knowing the child was her husband's, Mrs.

Rainer told Maria she could give birth to the baby, but she'd have to give it up for adoption if she wanted to keep her job. Maria had nowhere else to go, so she agreed. But, as the child grew in her belly, so did Maria's affection for him. After she gave birth, she refused to let the child go.

One night, while she was nursing her baby, Mr. Rainer came to her room and told her to get dressed. Forcing her to leave Troy in his cradle, he trundled Maria into his car. He drove them all night to Nuevo Laredo on the Texas/Mexico border. After abusing her one last time, he forced her out of the car and left her on the side of the road as he sped away. When border officials found her with no passport or green card, they deported her back to Mexico and she never saw Troy again.

When Troy finally found his mother, she told him that his father must have given him his surname and put him up for adoption. Maria shared how the border patrol returned her to Mexico and the struggles she'd faced after that to survive. Troy was heart-sick for his mother and made plans to travel to Mexico City to meet her in person, but Sterling had killed him before he had the chance. Maria Cortez was Beaux's only connection to Troy, and it had fallen on him to tell her she'd never get to see her son. Maria was inconsolable, and Beaux promised he would take care of her for Troy's sake.

He dialed the international number. "Maria? This is Beaux Crandall."

"Yes, Mr. Crandall. It is nice to hear your voice. I was just thinking about Troy and how lucky he was to have such a friend as you."

"I was the fortunate one. In fact, I've been missing

him a lot lately and reminiscing about the mischief we used to get into when we were boys."

"I wish he could have told me those stories. I'm broken-hearted that I didn't get to meet him after all the years of wondering and worrying, not knowing what happened to him."

"He was looking forward to meeting you, too. And trust my word." Beaux's stomach soured. "The man who killed him will pay for it with his own life one day."

"That will not bring our Troy back, Mr. Crandall."

"Please, call me Beaux. Your son was my best friend."

Maria's voice held reverence when she spoke his name. "Beaux."

"I called you this morning because I thought you might like to have some pictures of Troy. I don't have many, but I could email some to you if you will text me your email address." Beaux chewed his lip. He was lying. He had many photos of Troy and even more video, but the lucrative acts he'd been involved in at the time of shooting them were not something a mother wanted to see.

"I would love that, Mr. Crandall...Beaux. You are so kind. I don't know how to thank you."

"No need. I'll enjoy going through the images I have. It might take me a day or two."

"Thank you. I will treasure them."

Beaux signed off, and seconds later, a text with Maria's email, along with her home address, came through. He set his phone on a side table and rested his head against the chair. Wanting to rid himself of his grief, he stared down at Chinara. "Get busy. I'm counting on you to make me feel better, and I suggest you do a damn fine job."

The girl's fingers trembled as she pushed Beaux's robe to the side and bent to give him the pleasure he demanded. She had learned not to gag because that brought an immediate and harsh punishment. But until now, she refused to look at him. It was time to teach her to meet his gaze as she performed her task. He grabbed a handful of her hair and yanked her head back until her fear-filled eyes met his. Her gaze darted away, so he twisted her coarse curls in his fist, causing her to cry out.

"Look at me, you little bitch. And make me believe you love this," he growled. "You'll regret it if you disappoint me."

Her dark eyes, glossed with tears, shifted reluctantly to his face. Victory over the strong-willed girl filled him with deep satisfaction. When he was spent, she discreetly wiped her mouth with the back of her wrist. He released her hair, and she grabbed her top and scurried away.

7

———

Dirk and Hank had a short layover in Denver before they boarded their flight to Cheyenne. Teresa reserved a rental car for them at the Cheyenne airport and had texted Dirk the address for Ms. Katherine Downy, the woman who reported the stolen and abandoned car.

Hank drove, and by the time they got to Ms. Downy's house in a neighborhood south of the regional airport, there was no sign of the bright-red Cadillac anywhere. The police had probably confiscated the stolen vehicle when they left. Hank pulled to the curb of the older model brick home, and Dirk noted that though the house was built in the middle of the last century, the owner took good care of it. The lawn was browning in the fall weather, but someone kept the shrubs and walkways neatly trimmed.

Dirk surveilled the street and surrounding homes as they approached the front door. Everything was quiet and peaceful, as expected, in the middle of a weekday in suburbia. Hank rang the doorbell, and movement sounded from inside. The door swung open full-wide and an attractive woman in jeans and a western T-shirt looked out at them.

"Hello. Can I help you?"

Dirk appreciated the trust and openness that was still present in certain areas of the country. He held up his ID and brushed aside his leather jacket to reveal the silver star USMS badge he wore clipped to his belt.

"Ms. Downy, I'm Deputy US Marshal Sterling, and this is my partner, Deputy Flannigan. We'd like to talk with you about the car that you recently reported abandoned at your residence."

The woman's delicate brows pinched together. "I've already given a statement to the police. They impounded the car this morning. I don't know how else I can help."

"We believe the man who left the stolen car at your home is the same man we're trying to find. We just left California where we met with the woman who owns the car."

"Oh. Well, would you like to come in?"

"Thanks, Ms. Downy. That would be best." Dirk followed the woman to the small living room. She indicated they sit on the sofa against the wall.

"Please call me Katherine. Can I get you something to drink? Coffee maybe? I just made a fresh pot."

"Thanks, that'd be great." Dirk tried not to sound as desperate for the caffeine as he felt. "Hank?"

"Yes, please. Someone woke me way too early this

morning." Hank sent an engaging smile to Katherine, and she flushed as she left for the kitchen.

Dirk whispered, "Trying to charm the witness?"

"What?" Hank held his hand to his chest, feigning innocence. "I'm just letting her know we're friendly. You know—putting her at ease. Besides... she's cute."

Dirk smirked and shook his head.

"You have no room to talk after letting Missy Linden climb all over you yesterday." Hank shoved Dirk's shoulder.

"That was completely different." Dirk chuckled.

Katherine returned carrying a tray with three steaming cups of coffee, cream, sugar, and a plate of peanut butter cookies. "Here we are." Hank stood and helped her with the tray. She served them before taking her spot in an overstuffed chair facing them. After a long sip of coffee, she asked, "So, what do you want to know?"

Dirk took a sip of coffee. "What is the name of the man who left the car?"

"Don't you know? I thought you were looking for him."

Hank pulled a notepad and pen from his jacket pocket. "The man we're trying to find goes by many aliases."

Her brows knitted again. "My boyfriend—well, I guess he wasn't really my boyfriend after all—anyway, his name is Don Wise."

"And you were in a relationship with Mr. Wise?" Hank jotted notes in his book.

"Yes. At least I thought so. We'd been seeing each other for only a little over a week, but things moved fast.

We had an amazing connection right off the bat, and I thought it was a true sign of trust and a future that he would leave such a nice car with me when he went on his business trip." Katherine slid her hand over her mouth and shook her head. "I can't believe I was so stupid. I tried his phone number over and over when he didn't come back. I was terribly worried something had happened to him, like a car crash. Eventually, I realized he had left the car and did not plan to return. It wasn't until the police knocked on my door wondering why I had a stolen car in my driveway that I realized I'd been duped. I'm so embarrassed."

Hank leaned forward and touched her forearm. "You don't have any reason to be embarrassed. This guy is a professional con man. He did the same thing to the woman in LA. Did he ask you for anything else, like money?"

"No. Don seemed to always have cash. After our second date in two days, he stayed here in my house, but he never took anything. What is his real name?"

"If it's the same guy, and we're sure it is," Dirk rubbed his chin, "then his name is Simeon Gryms. Did he ever meet with anyone or receive any phone calls that you're aware of?"

"Not around me, but he must have. Otherwise, how would he have known he had to go on a business trip?" Dirk and Hank said nothing as reality worked its way through her thoughts. "Oh. Never mind. I guess on some level I still want to believe. Things seemed so good between us. I thought we had a future."

Hank gave her an understanding smile. "Too good to be true?"

"Obviously." Pink tinged her cheeks.

Dirk took a swig of coffee and set the cup and saucer on the table. "Did he mention anything about where he was going or what he planned to do when he got there? I realize most of what he told you was not honest, but sometimes when people lie, they mix in pieces of truth."

"He said he had to go back to the home office in Philadelphia. I dropped him off at the airport." Katherine took another pensive sip. "But he couldn't fly, could he? How would he get through security? If you guys are looking for him, isn't his name on a list with TSA? Do you think he had a fake ID?"

"I doubt he got on an airplane. His ID would have flagged, and there's also facial recognition software and so forth. He might have used a false ID to rent a car, or he could have had an accomplice pick him up." Dirk reached for one of the light, crispy cookies. It had the perfect peanut buttery flavor—clearly homemade. He rinsed the sweetness down with another swallow of coffee. "You said he left over a month ago? Any chance you know the exact date?"

"It was September twenty-seventh. I remember because it was my dad's birthday." Katherine's shoulders curled in. "I suppose you'll probably never find him now."

"Oh, we'll find him, ma'am." The confidence in Hank's voice made the corner of Dirk's mouth curl.

"Is there anything else you can think of Katherine?" Dirk asked.

"He told me he wanted to start his own business. To strike out on his own…" Her tone dropped. "He said we would do it together." She set her jaw, and determination glinted in her eyes. "I'll do anything to help you find him. To prevent other women from going through what the woman in California and I did. That man is a snake."

Dirk opened his wallet and handed her a business card. "If you think of anything else, or if you hear from him, please call me right away."

"Thank you. I will. I hope you find him."

Hank passed her his business card as well before they left the house. Dirk waited until they were in the car to give him crap. "You hoping she'll call you?"

"Just trying to be professional."

"Is that what that was? Professional what? Charmer?" Dirk laughed it off, but inside he was concerned. Things certainly weren't rosy for Hank and Amy at home. Was Hank looking for a diversion?

Hank ignored the question. "Where to from here, boss?"

"Teresa lined up a ride for us on a C-130 flying into Billings at three. Let's head over to the base." Dirk called Emory on the way.

Emory got straight to the point. "How did the interview go?"

Dirk's shoulders eased when he heard her voice. "It's definitely the same guy, but we didn't learn much. We think he might have rented a car at the airport. If so, we can track him. He left on September twenty-seventh. It's a decent lead. We need to search for a record of his car rental, and then we can find out where he dropped the car off."

"I'll get Teresa on that right away. Since this has been on the local news in Wyoming, we've had a handful of calls reporting sightings of Gryms. Who knows if any of them are reliable or not? We can chase those leads down this week." Her voice lowered to a whisper. "I miss you."

"Me too. I'll see you tonight."

8

Dirk and Hank signed in for space-A on the C-130 scheduled to fly from the Cheyenne Air National Guard base up to Billings. As promised, Teresa had all the details prearranged. They waited in flight ops to get final approval from the aircraft commander to get on the plane.

Dirk's phone buzzed with a call from Laurie. "Hey, what's up?"

"Just checking to see if you're still coming to dinner tonight?"

"That's the plan. I'm waiting to catch a hop up to Billings now. I should be there in a couple of hours. Does that work?"

"Perfectly. Caleb is excited to show you Bear's new tricks."

"I'm glad you let him keep that dog. Bear has been powerful medicine for Caleb."

"He has. I'm still grateful to Caitlyn for giving him to Caleb after Sam died. Having his own friend has helped him cope, and personally, I'm comforted knowing that Bear will protect Caleb no matter what."

"Yeah, Rottweilers are a great deterrent, even though they're big softies at heart."

"Bear is so funny. When Dave was here the other day and was playing with Caleb in the yard, Bear romped along, but kept himself between Caleb and Dave the entire time."

"Dave was there?" Dirk's stomach wrenched uncomfortably.

"He stopped by to drop off a scarf I accidentally left on my chair when I met him for coffee."

"When did that happen?" Dirk couldn't account for the edge in his voice. It wasn't jealousy. After all, he was the one who ended up with Emory, not Aldrich. Still, why couldn't the guy find someone to date outside of the women in Dirk's life?

"The other day. We just had coffee. That's okay, isn't it?" Laurie sounded apprehensive.

Dirk had no right to cast shade on her choices. "Yeah. Of course. See whomever you want. Do you need me to pick up anything on my way to your house?"

"I don't think so. I'll see you when you get here."

"Yeah, see you soon."

The paratrooper seats with their canvas straps weren't as comfortable as commercial airline chairs and there were no snacks, but there was plenty of leg room and it was only a little over an hour flight. Dirk and Hank clipped in for the powerful take-off and enjoyed the sway and dip of the four-engine turboprop as the pilots practiced low-level tactical flying through the mountains on their way north.

Dirk nudged Hank's shoulder. "Brings back memories, eh, kid?"

Hank bobbed his head. "Sure does, but I spent more time refueling off these bad boys than I did riding on them."

Hank had served as a helicopter pilot in Afghanistan during the war until enemy forces shot down his aircraft. He still struggled with survivor's guilt, though Dirk knew he was healing. After the crash, the kid had changed his MOS to 31A—Military Police. When he got out of the Army, he applied to the US Marshal Service, and Dirk was glad he did. Hank was sharp and proving to be an excellent partner.

"I spent my time jumping out of these babies when I was in the Corps." Dirk rested his head back against the silver hull and dozed, preferring not to recall the hundreds of missions he had been on. Those memories were dark and violent. And for the most part, he was able to keep them buried and under control.

It wasn't long before the C130 banked right and landed smoothly in Billings. Teresa was outside the hangar waiting to drive them back to the office where their private vehicles were. Dirk spotted her on the phone pacing next to her car gesturing with one hand and occasionally pressing her hand against her head. She was obviously upset, so Dirk picked up his pace.

She tossed her phone in her car just before they got to her. "Hey, T. What's going on? Everything alright? Is Tomas, okay?"

Teresa mumbled that everything was fine. "You guys are late."

"Yeah, sorry. No telling with a government flight. Was that call about Tomas?"

She sighed. "Yeah. They charge me extra if I'm late. Come on. Let's go."

Dirk and Hank climbed into her car. "Put the fee in your office expense report. It's our fault you were late. And next time, we can call an Uber."

"Don't worry about it. I've got it covered." She peeled out of the hangar's parking area.

"Whoa!" Hank snapped on his seatbelt. "Getting a ticket will only make you later." His tone was teasing, but Teresa didn't take it that way.

"Shut up, Flannigan. If I want your opinion... never mind, I don't."

Dirk and Hank hurried out of Teresa's car when she came to a stop next to their vehicles. Dirk leaned in. "Thanks for staying late, T. I'm sorry about being late, and we really do appreciate the ride."

"No problem. You owe me, though."

Dirk laughed. "And I have no doubt you'll collect."

Teresa raised her chin and drove away.

Dirk watched her taillights for a minute wondering if Teresa was okay. It wasn't like her to be so short. She was clearly dealing with a lot of stress. Single parenthood was tough. He pulled his helmet from the case attached to his Bonneville T120 and glanced at Hank. "You headed home?"

The muscles in Hank's jaw bunched as he clicked the

fob to unlock his truck. "Yep. Hopefully, Amy has had enough time to cool off. I guess we'll see."

"Take her some flowers or something." Dirk hated to see Hank miserable, too. His teammates were both struggling with their home lives.

"Couldn't hurt." Hank flashed him a grin that held no warmth and climbed into his truck. He started the grumbling diesel engine and drove out of the lot.

Dirk was thankful the weather remained mild. Winter could show up any day in the Montana autumn, but so far, an Indian Summer held on and made for a relaxing ride out to Laurie's house. As he rode, his mind sifted through memories of Sam. They had been close friends. Dirk's chest expanded with warmth, and he smiled, remembering the hundreds of dinners he'd shared with Sam and Laurie over the years. And at how much it had meant to him when they asked him to be Caleb's godfather. When he and Sam linked up with Caitlyn Reed, they used to joke about their team being the Three Musketeers with a dog.

Their Chief Deputy hadn't assigned him to the case that killed Sam. His partner had been working with Caitlyn and her K9 partner, Renegade, at the time, but she'd been on a day off when the courthouse in Mammoth exploded, killing Sam and the judge they were trying to protect. Caitlyn insisted she should have been there that day instead of Sam, and Dirk wished he had been too. Sam had left behind a wife and a little kid. Dirk didn't have anyone who would have cared. It made no sense. It wasn't fair.

Dirk blinked against the sudden blur in his vision and

pressed on the accelerator. His motorcycle sailed over the highway, whisking him away from the sad memories. He exited the freeway and glided through the suburban neighborhood to the Dillinger house. Caleb was in the front yard throwing a stick for Bear when he pulled into the driveway.

"Unka Dirk!" the boy shouted and ran toward him.

Dirk slid off his helmet and swung his leg over the bike. He reached to lift Caleb up for a hug. Bear barked and bounced with excitement. "Hey, buddy. Looks like you and Bear are having fun." Dirk scratched Bear's black and brown head with his free hand. "Good boy."

Laurie stepped out on the porch and waved. A glimpse of what it might be like to come home to a beautiful wife and adoring kid—a family of his own—flashed through his mind, but he quickly dismissed it. He'd had his chance for that with Hannah, and he'd made a mess of it. They both did. Getting through the wreckage of his life after their baby died, and then finding Hannah consoling herself by sleeping with his best friend, was the darkest time in his existence. Dirk had lost the three people that meant the most to him in the course of a couple of months. He had barely survived and would never set himself up to be that vulnerable ever again.

"Dinner will be ready in about twenty minutes," Laurie called.

"Sounds good." Dirk shook off his painful memories. "Caleb and I will do our best to tire Bear out until then." Dirk set Caleb on his feet and climbed off the bike. He pulled off his black leather jacket and tossed it across the saddle.

Dirk threw the stick for Bear to chase and then crouched down on Caleb's level. As a reward, the boy tried to tackle him. Dirk played along and fell over, bringing Caleb to the ground with him. He pretended to wrestle with the little guy, allowing Caleb to pin him down. Bear returned with the stick but dropped it on the grass in favor of licking Dirk's face instead.

"Hey, this is two against one!" Dirk laughed. Playing with Caleb was the only time Dirk truly relaxed. The three of them chased each other around the yard until Laurie called them in to wash up.

Dirk held Caleb up to the sink and they sudsed up their hands. He drew in a long savory breath through his nose. "Something sure smells good."

"Beef Stroganoff." Laurie set a large, steaming serving dish in the center of the table.

Before dinner, Caleb fed Bear, spilling half the scoop of dog food all over the floor.

"It's okay. Bear likes it that way." Caleb beamed, proud of accomplishing his chore as his dog lapped up the loose kibble.

The look on Caleb's face warmed Dirk's heart.

LAURIE FILLED their water glasses as she watched Dirk and Caleb. "I never see you laugh any other times like you do when you're playing with Caleb." Laurie brushed dried leaves from Dirk's shirt as she walked by. She also noticed the way Bear responded to him. The dog obviously felt no need to protect Caleb from Dirk. She remembered the week after Sam's funeral when Caitlyn Reed brought Bear to their house. He was a puppy then, and Caitlyn wanted Caleb to have him. She told Laurie then that she should always trust their dog's instincts. Smiling at the thought, Laurie continued, "It's nice to hear the sound. You seem happy."

Dirk didn't respond to her observation. He helped settle Caleb in his booster seat and then sat in the chair next to him. He never took Sam's place at the head of the table.

"I hope you're hungry. I made a ton."

"I'm always hungry." Dirk offered her his usual half smile.

"How was your trip?"

"Informative. We have some solid leads on a guy we're trying to find." Dirk took a big bite of gravy covered meat and noodles. After he swallowed, he sipped his drink and asked, "You mentioned you had coffee with Aldrich? How did that go?"

"It was fun. He's going to take me to dinner on Friday." Laurie watched Dirk's face as he carefully cloaked his expression. "You don't approve?"

"It's not for me to approve or disapprove. It's your life."

A wave of defensiveness rose in Laurie's chest. "You don't like him. Is it because of his past relationship with Emory?"

"There might be some of that. Honestly, I think Aldrich is a good enough guy. I just don't get why he can't find somebody to date that I don't know."

"You have to admit, you sound a little jealous." Laurie

grinned at him in a teasing manner. "But don't worry because to tell the truth, I sometimes think Dave's more interested in your team than in me. He's always asking questions about what you guys are doing at work."

"Ha! The dude probably wishes he was a deputy marshal rather than some FBI dweeb." Dirk chuckled.

"You don't think he might have leftover feelings for Emory?" Laurie swiped up a drop of the rich wine and mushroom sauce from her placemat to cover her concern.

"Nah. Sounds like he's moved on to me. He's probably just trying to find something you two have in common to talk about."

After dinner, Dirk helped Laurie gather the plates while Caleb played with Bear in the living room. Laurie filled the dish sink with hot sudsy water.

"When are you ever gonna get a dishwasher in this place?" Dirk asked.

"The expense is not a priority right now. It's just Caleb and me, and we don't use that many dishes."

Dirk washed while Laurie dried, and when the kitchen was clean, Dirk helped Caleb get into his pajamas and read him a bedtime story. While they did that, Laurie cut two pieces of pie and made a pot of coffee.

When Dirk came back to the living room, Laurie handed him a mug. "Thanks for putting Caleb to bed. It's nice to have a break."

"I love doing it." A shadow haunted his eyes, and Laurie figured he was thinking about his own little boy, who died so young. Dirk carried more pain in his heart than he ever let anyone know about. She wished she could ease his burden in some way and was glad that spending time with Caleb brought him comfort.

"I made cherry pie. Would you like a piece?"

"Absolutely. But I can't stay long. I'm stopping by Emory's after this."

Laurie still felt a tinge of envy at the look in Dirk's eyes when he spoke of Emory. Other than Sam, Dirk was the best man she knew. She had desperately wanted to have a deeper relationship with him, but he had fallen in love with his boss.

Laurie handed Dirk his pie, and she curled up on the end of the couch with her own plate. "How's your other investigation going? The Crandall thing?"

"I'm still trying to locate him, but Emory wants Hank and me working on this recent case for now. So any investigating I do is on my own time."

"Do you think you'll ever find him?"

"I won't stop hunting for him until I do."

9

———

Hank took Dirk's advice and stopped to buy Amy some flowers on his way home. He parked in the lot of their apartment complex and kicked through a bunch of colorful dried autumn leaves covering the walkway to the building. It had been a long two days, and he was glad to be back and looked forward to seeing his pregnant wife. He couldn't believe they would be a threesome by this time next year.

He unlocked the door, and as he entered the apartment, he called out, "Hey babe, I'm home!"

There was no answer. He knew she was there because he'd seen her car outside. "Amy?" he shouted.

He heard her voice coming from the bedroom. She was on the phone and sounded upset. Hank dropped his bag by the door, and carrying the roses, he rushed to their room. Amy lay curled up on the bed, holding the device to her ear. Tears streamed from her eyes. Hank's heart wrenched, and he reached for her in concern. He caressed her shoulder and tried to catch her eye, but she turned away from him, burying her face in the pillow.

Hank didn't know what made her so upset, but he sat in the chair across the room to wait until she was ready to talk to him.

"He's home. I have to go," Amy sniffled. "I'll call you later."

"What's the matter, sweetheart? Are you okay?" Hank leaned forward, bracing his elbows on his thighs. The bouquet dangled from his hand.

Amy pulled her knees up to her chest and narrowed her red eyes. "I hate it when you're gone. When you wanted to become a deputy marshal, I had no idea it would mean so much travel. You spend more time with Dirk Sterling than you do with me."

"Amy, that's not true." Hank released a sigh that sounded more like a groan. "I'm sorry there's been more travel than we expected, but it's not like criminals stay in one place making it easy for us to catch them."

"Catching criminals is more important to you than I am—than our baby is!"

Her accusation made no sense to him. "How can you say that? I love you, Amy." He held up the flowers and gave them a shake, rattling the plastic cover and sending their sweet scent through the air. "See, I brought you roses. I love you both. But I also have a job. It's how I will provide for you and our baby. I do not care more about the criminals than you." Hank moved to sit on the side of the bed next to her, but she curled into herself even tighter. "Do you want a cup of tea? It might help you feel better. Or can I get you something to eat?"

Amy buried her face in her knees and cried. Hank didn't know what to do to comfort her. He tried to wrap his arms around her, but she rolled away from him.

"What's going on, Amy? Why are you so upset. This can't be good for the baby. Should you call your doctor?"

She glared up at him from under wet spiky lashes. "This is not a medical issue, Hank. This is about us."

"I thought we were doing better—working things out. But you seem more emotional than ever, and I don't know what I did." He stood up and paced to the bathroom door, choking on his frustration. He jammed his hands into his pants pockets and turned back toward his wife. "I thought everything would be fine now that you are pregnant. This is what you said you wanted. And yet, you're still miserable. I don't know what to do."

Amy reached for a box of tissues on her nightstand. She wiped her eyes, blew her nose, and hiccupped. "Getting pregnant didn't solve anything, Hank."

"Obviously." He swallowed his sarcasm and took a steadying breath. "Look, I'm not sure what needs to be solved. Can you help me out a little?" His tone communicated his utter exasperation. "What do you want me to do?"

"Don't yell at me."

"You are so frustrating! I'm not yelling. I just don't understand what's going on with you. Who were you talking to on the phone?"

"My mother—not that it's any of your business."

"Was she able to give you any helpful advice?" He doubted it. His mother-in-law caused more trouble than not.

Amy ignored his question and crawled off the bed. She padded into the bathroom, where she splashed cold water on her face. The action helped her to stop crying, but her cheeks remained blotchy with emotion. Hank's chest ached with sympathy and confusion. He hated seeing his wife so upset, especially when it seemed there was nothing he could do to comfort her.

"How about I make us something for dinner? Maybe a little food will help you feel better and then we can talk. It kills me to see you so sad. I feel helpless."

"If you really wanted to help me," Amy spoke to his reflection in the mirror, "you would find a different job."

The familiar surge of anger seared Hank's retort, sealing the bitter words inside his throat. They had been over this countless times. Leaving his career was not an option. "How does a tuna melt sound? I'm starving. It's been a long day." Hank turned away from her and walked down the hall toward the kitchen.

By the time Hank finished cooking the sandwiches, Amy joined him at the bar between the kitchen and the living room. She slid onto a barstool, and Hank handed her a plate with her hot sandwich and some chips. He sat next to her with his meal, and they ate in silence. His food tasted like paste.

When he finished eating, he wiped his mouth with a paper napkin and reached for her hand. "Have you talked to your doctor about feeling depressed? Do you think maybe all of this has to do with your hormones?"

Amy's eyes shot arrows of fury at him, and she jumped to her feet. "How dare you blame all our problems on my hormones! That is so patronizing. Why can't you take any responsibility for how you make me feel?"

Hank's mouth fell open, but no words came. He was stunned at her accusation when he was only trying to help. Amy stormed down the hall, slamming their bedroom door behind her. His aggravation made him want to throw his plate across the room just to hear it crash. Instead, he took a deep, calming breath, and letting it out slowly, he cleaned up their dishes. When he was done, he pulled some shorts, a T-shirt, and his running shoes out of his luggage and changed clothes in the living room before leaving for a long run.

With each pounding footfall, Hank released his tension. He hadn't meant to offend Amy with his question about hormones, but her volatile emotions made no sense to him. He couldn't help but wonder if her hormones played a role in this mess. Maybe he should call the doctor and ask the questions himself. There had to be something he could do better. Something that would comfort his wife besides leaving his career.

10

Teresa sped away from the Marshals building parking lot, her stomach tight with anxiety. It was bad enough she had to pay money she didn't have because she was so late in picking up Tomas, but how must her son feel? The only kid left at the after-school care center, alone with his caregiver for over an hour. If only she would have known the plane wasn't on time. She could have picked him up before she drove out to get the guys.

"Damn it!" She slammed her hand against the steering wheel when the traffic light ahead turned red. "Come on. Come on. Come ON!"

She sped through the neighborhood streets and flew into the elementary school parking lot. Leaving her car at the curb, she ran to the locked door. Groaning, she rang the bell.

"Yes?" A tinny voice rattled through the speaker.

"Teresa Mendez, to pick up Tomas in afterschool care."

The door buzzed, and Teresa yanked it open. She dashed to the gymnasium where the kids usually were when it was time to get them. The gym was dark. Where was her son? She ran into the hall, trying to guess where he might be. Maybe she should wait there.

"Hello?" Teresa called into the empty halls.

"Mom!" Tomas ran toward her from the art room.

"Hey, buddy. I'm sorry I wasn't here on time! I had to pick up Mr. Dirk and Mr. Hank from the airport and their plane was late."

"It's okay. I got to make a clay bear."

A young woman she hadn't met before followed Tomas down the hall at a slower pace. She was as thin as a reed in her flowing airy dress and wore her blond hair in two long straight braids. "Hi. I'm Ms. Frieza. The art teacher."

"Oh." Teresa didn't like that her son was with a woman she didn't know. Even if she was a teacher at his school. "Where is Ms. Brown?"

"She had an appointment and had to leave."

"Without telling me?"

"Well, you were rather late."

"Still. She should inform me of a staff change." Teresa's agitation stirred, but she didn't want to take out her stress on the woman who was kind enough to stay with Tomas. "But thank you very much for being here. It was an unforeseeable situation."

"It happens. Don't worry. Tomas and I had fun, didn't we, kiddo?" Ms. Frieza ruffled Tomas's black hair with a familiarity that rubbed against Teresa's nerves.

"Yeah!" He turned his dark brown eyes to her. "Ms.

Frieza is gonna cook my bear in the oven, then I can bring it home!"

The teacher laughed fondly. "In a kiln."

"Yeah, a kiln!"

Teresa inserted a brightness she did not feel into her voice. "That's great. I can't wait to see it. You ready to go? I bet you're starved."

"Nah, I'm okay. Ms. Frieza gave me a snack."

"Oh—good." She guessed. "Well, thank you again. Come on, Tomas. We've already taken up too much of Ms. Frieza's time. Grab your pack and let's go."

Her son turned and waved at the woman, who was clearly his new favorite teacher. They got into the car, and Teresa sat for a few seconds breathing her stress under control. She didn't have to race anymore, but her body still hummed as though she did.

"Mom, can we go to McDonalds?"

Her stomach knotted tighter. Such a simple request. Most parents would give in, especially on a night like this, but she couldn't afford another twenty bucks for dinner. "No, sweetie. Let's get home. I'll make you a grilled cheese. How does that sound?"

"We always have grilled cheese," Tomas grumbled.

"I know bud. I'm sorry." She was failing at the single mom thing. Everything was so expensive. The clinic and antibiotics for Tomas's strep throat were not in the budget, and the grocery bill shocked her every time she shopped, and she barely bought the necessities. Thank God she could claim her gas mileage at work, but lately she'd been missing hours in the office and didn't feel as though she could say no when the Chief asked her for a couple of extra hours at the end of a day. But instead of earning more, it ended up costing her in childcare. God, it seemed like her life was in a downward spiral that spun faster and faster. She couldn't breathe.

Teresa pulled into the carport of her tiny one-bedroom house, which had worked for them when Tomas was a toddler, but the walk-in closet she used for his bedroom was too small now. She thought about selling, but with the price of real estate skyrocketing, she couldn't afford a bigger place. The best solution she could come up with was to get a sleeper sofa. She could use the living room and let Tomas have the bedroom.

"Did you get your homework done?"

"Yeah."

Teresa chose to believe him. She was too tired to deal with it, anyway. "Good. Let's get you some supper. It won't be long before it's bedtime."

Once Tomas was finally asleep, Teresa collapsed on her bed, her mind racing. She needed a raise but couldn't ask for one right now. Not when she had been the one to ask for less responsibility. She'd begged to set aside her badge and become the office admin so she could be home for Tomas, and that position came with far less pay. And lately she'd been missing work, too, so there was no way she could justify asking for more money.

She needed sleep, but the rest was elusive as her mind sifted through all the ways she was failing and coming up with no solid solutions. The mortgage was due again in another week, and they were low on groceries. There was no way out. She couldn't get a second job because she couldn't afford to pay anyone to watch Tomas. If she knew where Tomas's father was, she could force him to pay child support, but he had disappeared before she knew she was pregnant, and besides, Teresa didn't want to risk having to share her son with a basic stranger. No, it was her and Tomas against the world, and the world was winning.

11

The evening had turned cool, and Emory clicked on her gas fireplace. She breathed in the musky sweet scent of her Cabernet before sipping the black-cherry toned wine and studied the research document that filled the screen on her laptop. Emory was determined to catch Simeon Gryms. His arrest and incarceration were a necessary feather in her cap as the Chief US Deputy Marshal in Billings. Gradually, thanks to her fantastic team, she was building a solid reputation in the USMS.

Emory glanced at her watch. She expected Dirk any minute, and it was getting hard to concentrate on work. It had been a long while since they had set time aside for each other. And even when they had time, Dirk remained preoccupied with hunting down Beaux Crandall. She had her doubts they'd ever locate him. The criminal mastermind could be anywhere in the world. Emory figured it was better to chase after criminals she was certain they could find, and Simeon was such a man.

Gryms began his career in crime as a con man. He became notorious for his ability to woo wealthy women and make them fall in love with him. They invariably invited him to move into their homes and paid for his expenses. In return, he made them feel loved and less lonely. When he tired of a particular woman he lived with, he would rob her of her jewels and any other valuables she kept at home before moving on to his next unsuspecting victim.

All of that was bad enough, but recently Gryms upped the ante by holding up an armored truck in Denver. Emory wondered at the massive leap from con artist to armed robbery and murder. What had precipitated the change? Obviously, he was desperate for cash, but since he shot a guard during the robbery, he was now involved in a homicide, too. After he killed the guard, Gryms escaped in a bright-red Cadillac coupe. Yesterday, Dirk and Hank had interviewed the California woman to whom the car belonged, and gathered detailed information about Gryms they didn't know before.

Earlier, the men spoke with a woman in Wyoming, who had also fallen for Gryms's con. Later, he disappeared, leaving her with the stolen Cadillac. Gryms's last known location was Cheyenne, Wyoming. He had been traveling north from Denver and could be anywhere by now. Emory suspected he was hiding out in one of the upper western states. Since Gryms traveled north from Denver after the robbery, Emory figured he was likely hiding in Wyoming, possibly Montana, or even the Dakotas, and she focused her entire team's efforts on finding him.

The loud roar of a motorcycle cut into the quiet night. Emory recognized the sound of Dirk's bike, and her insides revved in harmony with the engine. On her way to greet him, she checked her hair and make-up in the mirror. After brushing a few stray strands into place and pinching some color into her cheeks, she opened the door.

Warmth bloomed in her belly as his boots sounded on the stairs. Dirk rounded the corner, his dark eyes burning with hunger as he strode toward her. He slid his fingers into her hair at her temples and drew her into a sizzling kiss.

"Hello." He murmured as he nuzzled her neck.

Emory giggled. "Hello to you too." She brushed his cheek with her lips and took his hand, leading him into her apartment. "How was dinner?"

"Fine. It's always good to spend time with Caleb."

"Just Caleb? How is Laurie?"

"She's fine. Did you know she and Aldrich are dating now?"

"No. I haven't spoken with Dave in a long time. I knew he wanted to ask her out but didn't know he had. So, things are going well with them?" Emory watched Dirk's face closely, but he gave her no emotional tells.

"I guess. He's taking her to dinner on Friday."

"Does that bother you?" Emory reached to remove Dirk's jacket, and she hung it in the small closet by the front door.

"Not really. At least not in the way you're suggesting. It seems strange, that's all. But if Laurie likes him, I'll get used to it." Dirk crossed the room and stared at her open laptop screen. "You're as bad as me—working all the time. Find anything new?"

"No. Just more information to back up what we already know. How did your interview with Katherine Downy go today?"

"I felt sorry for her. I don't know what this guy has that so many women want, but they sure seem willing to give him everything they own."

"I think he takes advantage of their loneliness."

"I suppose. Hank seemed to hit it off with her. Must be the sense of vulnerability."

"Too bad for her he's married."

"Mmm."

"Do you have any inkling where Gryms might be hiding out?"

"Could be anywhere—Wyoming, Montana. These states are big and have tons of open space to hide in. But when he runs out of money, I suspect he'll go back to financing his life via his original MO. If he does, he'll have to land somewhere he can find a wealthy woman willing to put up with him. If we stick with that theory, my guess would be the areas around Bozeman, or even Missoula. That's where the big money is. What are your thoughts?"

Emory poured Dirk a glass of wine and brought it to him. "I agree with you. Where will you start?"

Dirk took a large sip of Cabernet and then raised one black brow. "I'd like to start with you assigning this job to Hank and Teresa and letting me pursue the Crandall case."

"I know that's what you want. But let's get this win

before we work backwards. That makes sense, doesn't it? We're very close to catching Gryms. I can feel it. Let's focus on him for now. Besides, you have no idea where on earth Crandall is. Right now, it's a cold case."

"It's only cold because you won't let me keep it hot. In my personal time, I've been looking into Crandall's history and the backgrounds of those who worked for him. Especially his bodyguard, Troy Rainer. The two were childhood friends. There might be something there. It's rare for someone to disconnect completely from everything in their lives, even when they're trying to hide."

"We know Crandall and Rainer grew up in the social system. Once they were teens, they spent most of their time in juvenile hall. Other than themselves, what connections could they have maintained?"

"That's what I'd like to find out. Social Services might have placed them in families that Beaux cared about. Or there could be other foster kids he still has a relationship with. Who knows? But the only way I can figure it out is if you'll let me investigate."

There were two reasons Emory wasn't encouraging Dirk's investigation into Crandall right now. The obvious one was that she had prioritized Gryms over Crandall for the sake of her career, and second, she didn't want to appear as though she was favoring Dirk over the other deputies on her team. Their inner office relationship made her nervous. She never wanted it to appear as though Dirk had any undue influence over her, or as though she made decisions involving the team that favored him.

"You'll have plenty of time to investigate Crandall once we apprehend Gryms." Emory slid her arms around his waist and pressed her cheek against his broad back. At the moment, she did not want to be his boss. She much preferred the role of lover. "Besides, you didn't really come over here tonight to discuss fugitives, did you?" She smiled at the deep chuckle that rumbled in his chest.

He turned within the circle of her arms to face her and lifted her chin. "No. The last thing I want to do is talk about work." He set down his wineglass before taking hers. He placed it next to his, and then took her hand and led her to the bedroom.

Yet even as he kissed her and unbuttoned her blouse, she sensed his pre-occupation. His restless mind wanted to pick up a thread that would lead him to Crandall.

12

Beaux gazed across the sun-dappled sea at the massive, elegant yacht approaching his dock. Excitedly, he wrung his hands and glanced back towards his merchandise, all lined up and prepared to greet his visitors. The young women and children who belonged to him dressed in festive Ankara clothing. The girls wore flowers in their hair. Also awaiting his guests, was his fleet of servants in crisp, white cotton uniforms, standing at the ready to meet every need and desire.

The marble veranda of his beachside mansion was prepared for their important business meeting. The men and one woman who arrived represented politicians from various countries and wealthy business leaders from around the world. Beaux invited each one as a potential investor in his new venture. The drugs, firearms, and prostitution sections of his enterprise were easy enough to set up and finance, but Beaux dreamed of more.

While he was in Montana—when Troy was still alive

—they had come up with the idea of a subscription-based pornography and snuff film site. Beaux was giddy thinking of the constant stream of income for evergreen digital products that such a venture would bring. Now, all he had to do was convince the people floating toward him to invest in this lucrative opportunity. His challenge was to set up his business on the dark web in such a way that it could never lead back to him. He would have to hire someone to do that highly specialized work. But who could he trust?

As the yacht drew closer, Beaux saw his potential business partners enjoying mimosas on the deck. Sea gulls flapped their silver-white wings in the sky above and squawked *keow*, *keow*, hoping for signs of food. The seagoing passengers were all dressed in various combinations of the same exquisitely tailored linen suits with crisp white shirts and straw Panama hats. These guests were customers of his business when he was in Montana. Now he hoped to convince them to become investors. Beaux walked to the end of the pier to greet them as the crew hopped from the craft to secure it to the dock. Sailors clamped a set of steps to the edge of the yacht, and the visitors looked past Beaux to peruse the selection he offered as they descended the stairs.

"Welcome. Welcome." Beaux shook each of their hands as they stepped onto the boardwalk. "It's a great pleasure to have you here in my humble home. Refreshments are awaiting you on the veranda. Please, come this way."

Sweat trickled down Beaux's forehead, not merely

because of his girth in the heat, but also in anticipation of the outcome of this meeting and how it could secure his future. If only Troy was here to enjoy it with him. He strode up the beach toward his mansion at a measured pace, allowing his guests to consider the variety of his merchandise and their impending enjoyment with it. Several men stopped along the way to dally with their fantasies.

Beaux turned and held his hands together, hoping to express a patience he did not have. "Come now, honored guests. There will be plenty of time for that. After our meeting, you have the entire weekend to fulfill all your desires. But let's get the business out of the way first, and then nothing will hold you back from your enjoyment."

Reluctantly, the men and woman followed him. At the top of the beach, Beaux led them over a winding sand path through natural grasses leading to his opulent home. The sweet scent of flowering tropical vines perfumed the humid air. On the veranda, servants awaited them with cold drinks, fresh fruit, and pastries. Staff directed his guests to sit on cushions around a low table—Roman style—under fans blowing a misty spray that kept them cool.

Beaux provided each visitor with their own individual servant to attend them, and once everyone was served and comfortable, he began his presentation. On an enormous TV screen mounted on the wall behind him, Beaux showed carefully selected clips from his pornography collection. Once he had everyone's attention, he moved on to films that included children. He observed the men and woman as they viewed the content. Some were visibly excited and stimulated. Others appeared to turn away. But then watched surreptitiously from behind their drinks or food. This told Beaux exactly what he needed to know.

He paused the video at a particularly provocative scene. "This is a brief sample of the types of products I am able to offer on the dark web. Not all of you enjoy watching such things, and that is understandable. We all have our own fetishes. Many customers wish to experience more intense versions than I am displaying for you this morning. If you would like to view my full selection, it is all available to you in the privacy of your individual suites. However, all of you can imagine the income such films will bring.

"Before I arrived here, I ran an extremely lucrative enterprise in the United States. Unfortunately, my business was... interrupted. I am now in the process of rebuilding. I have plans to double or even triple the profit I was making there. And in order to do that, I need financial backing."

All eyes shifted to him then. This was the opportunity they traveled here to discuss whether or not they approved of the delights Beaux provided. They all understood how much money there was to be made.

"The films I will not show at this time are the products that will bring in the most money. I am sure you've heard of a product appropriately termed 'snuff' film. Before I left the United States, I had only one of those videos to offer, and it alone made me over a million dollars within weeks of production. In this location, there is far greater and less complicated access to a selection of characters I can choose to star in these films. Not to mention, fewer regulations on my activities. Imagine the money we could make if we joined together in this venture."

The man sitting farthest away from him at the back of the room took a long sip from his umbrella drink. "What is it you are asking from us, Crandall? On the way up the beach, we saw that you have many *actors* available for your films. I can see you also have plenty of private locations to film on your island. What else do you require?"

"Yes, I have all of that in place. Those things are easy." Beaux waved dismissively. "Now, I need top-of-the-line filming equipment and a talented crew I can trust. I also need a technician who can build a computer program through which I can offer these films and that is able to securely maintain a subscription service. Obviously, this is very sensitive work, and it will cost me—us—a great deal of money. However, once we're up and running, your investment will quickly return ten or twentyfold and at times even more. There is no cap to the amount of money we can make together."

"Along with financing, you also need help to locate the appropriate personnel?" asked a slight man to Beaux's left who couldn't seem to tear his eyes from the scene still frozen on the screen.

"Exactly. I believe the quality of expertise I need can only come from people with your degree of wealth and agency. Obviously, I put myself at great personal risk, sharing my hopes and dreams with you. But I trust I can count on your confidentiality, whether or not you choose to participate in making millions, perhaps even billions, of dollars with me. You wouldn't have come here if you weren't interested in enjoying what I have to offer."

The guests fell silent as they considered the financial opportunity that lay before them. Beaux's servants stepped in to provide any form of comfort those around the table required. After twenty minutes of refilling drinks and plates, and whispering amongst themselves, the oldest man in the group stood.

"This is a very intriguing offer, Crandall. One in which we can all envision the scale of financial benefit." He chuckled and spread his hand toward a beautiful servant woman. "And the obvious fringe benefits as well. I have in my employ such a technician who could build the programming you require. However, with blunt and open honesty, I would estimate the cost for his services in building such a program to be around twelve to fifteen million US dollars. I don't know what your projected cost for film equipment and so forth is, but it seems pertinent to discuss the numbers."

Beaus felt the blood drain from his face. He hadn't expected such a high number for the computer program, though he knew he'd have to pay dearly for the type of confidentiality his business venture required. He had already spent most of the money he had in his offshore accounts to buy his island and procure his workers. That meant he needed one-hundred percent funding for his dream. Would the people gathered here agree to such an investment?

Patting the moisture gathering on his brow, Beaux bought a few seconds by drinking some vodka-spiked pineapple juice. "We will all become exceedingly profitable with an initial investment of twenty million dollars —four million apiece from each of you. Considering the potential, it is a relatively small investment, and with the subscription format, the money just keeps flowing in. Globally, pornography is a ninety-seven billion a year industry. I believe we should enjoy a cut of that, don't you?"

"Lady and gentlemen, we are on the precipice of a great joint venture. Please consider the numbers in these folders. I'm eager to hear what you think." Beaux nodded to a servant at his side. The young man passed out packets which lined out the details of the money necessary for the deal. Beaux held his breath as he gauged his guests' responses to the information.

They sipped their drinks while they read through the financial figures and murmured amongst themselves in their various languages. Coming to a tentative agreement of some sort, one man stood to speak.

"Mr. Crandall, your deal is highly intriguing, and we are all positively inclined. However, we would like some time to think it over. Perhaps we could gather again at the end of the day tomorrow to discuss our conclusions?"

Beaux had hoped to have a deal in place before he allowed them free rein in his playground. But he was prepared for his guests to ask for some time and the delicacies he had to offer would only help to secure their investment.

"Of course." Beaux spread his arms out wide. "Your servants will show you to your suites. Please, make yourselves comfortable, and know that anything, *anything at all,* you desire is but a breath away. There is nothing you cannot have or do on my magical island. On your way to your rooms, feel free to select your first companion from my collection, or companions, if you so choose. Enjoy yourselves and I look forward to meeting with you again tomorrow evening at dinner."

13

———

Dirk tapped at his keyboard with irritation. He'd been following supposed leads that came in via the phone number posted on the news broadcast for anyone who might have seen Simeon Gryms. Hundreds of calls had come in, and so far, none of them led them anywhere concrete. Dirk hated this part of the job. It was pure desk-bound hell. He needed a break.

"I'm going to go grab some lunch. Anyone want to come?" He announced to the room at large.

Hank shrugged. "I'm not really hungry." He hunched further over his computer keyboard.

"I'll go with you." Teresa pushed back from her desk. She poked her head into Emory's office. "Dirk and I are grabbing lunch. Want us to pick you up anything while we're out?"

"No, thank you. I brought food so I could work through the lunch hour. There are so many calls to sift through. It's kind of overwhelming."

"Okay, we'll be back in a little bit."

Teresa followed Dirk to the elevators and out of the building. They didn't speak until they were sitting inside Dirk's black Jeep Rubicon. He started the engine and then canted his head to face her. "Don't you think it's a waste of time to have everyone in the office going through these pointless phone calls?"

"The calls are only pointless if none of them lead anywhere. It only takes one, and the only way we can find the one is to go through each of them."

"True, but I should hunt down Crandall at the same time. Having all four of us do the same job is a waste of time." Dirk pulled out of the parking lot and headed downtown. "Where do you want to eat?"

They ended up at their favorite burger joint. Before they ordered, Teresa asked, "Should we get our food to-go and take it back to work? I feel guilty sitting here with the chief and Hank stuck at the office, slaving away."

"No way. I need a decent break before I can stare at my computer screen for an entire afternoon filled with brain numbing minutiae. This case isn't very exciting." Dirk ordered a Philly cheesesteak with sweet potato fries and a beer. Teresa ordered a small burger and fries with water, but when she went to pay, she was short on cash. Dirk covered the tab.

Teresa's complexion darkened. "Thanks. I thought I had a twenty."

"No problem. I told you I owed you one, anyway. This might be the last warm day we have in a long while, want to sit outside?"

Teresa followed him to a table in the sun. "I know

you've been going against the chief's orders and working on your investigation of Beaux Crandall when she's not looking. Have you had any luck? Any idea where he is?"

He crunched a sweet crispy fry and grinned at being caught. "Nothing yet. I've been delving into his childhood. There's got to be a clue that points me in the right direction."

"Good luck when the boss catches on to what you're up to." Teresa took a big bite of her burger, wiping at a drip of greasy juice that trailed down her chin. She swallowed the mouthful down with a gulp of water. "What's going on with Hank today? I've never seen him turn down food before."

"I don't know. Still having trouble at home, I think."

"Poor guy. I thought things were getting better now that they're pregnant."

"Goes to show. A baby doesn't fix anything."

"Yeah. I'm living proof of that."

"Maybe, but you're a great mom, Teresa. Tomas is lucky to have you."

Teresa waved away the compliment and sucked loudly at her straw until the remaining drops of her drink were gone. "I'm going to go get a refill." Her chair scraped on the cement as she stood.

"While you're at it, order a couple of burgers to go." Dirk handed her his credit card.

Teresa lifted a dark brow. "Still hungry?"

"No, it's for Hank."

"Good idea. Hank needs to eat whether he's hungry or not." She took her cup and went to order.

Dirk used the opportunity to check his phone

messages. Marco Agosti, his contact from Interpol, had left a message. Marco hadn't been able to find any sign of Crandall setting up business anywhere, but he promised to keep an eye out and let Dirk know if he discovered anything of interest. Dirk was eager to get back to his search poking around in Crandall's childhood and that of Crandall's best friend, Troy Rainer.

When they returned to the office, Dirk didn't pretend to work on the Gryms case. He started immediately with a search through both Beaux Crandall's and Troy Rainer's legitimate banking histories, hoping to find trails to less obvious accounts. As he suspected, Crandall's financial web was massive. Hundreds of transfers to questionable accounts and banks located overseas. The FBI had forensic accountants going through that information, but Dirk was looking for something else. Something more personal. A clue to where the man scurried off to hide.

An hour later, after not finding anything useful, he switched over to Rainer's account. The difference was shocking. First of all, Rainer had only one account he could find. Twice a month, Troy received a deposit from one of Crandall's fake businesses. And second, starting a little over a year ago, there was an electronic funds transfer scheduled once a month that went from Troy's account to a bank in Mexico. Upon further investigation, Dirk determined that the bank in Mexico was legitimate, as was the account receiving the money.

The Mexican account was in the name of a woman called Maria Cortez, and the branch she banked with was in Mexico City. There had been no attempt to disguise the transfer, the account, or the owners of the accounts.

Either Rainer wasn't smart enough to cover his tracks, or he didn't think he needed to. This could be the clue Dirk was searching for.

Who was this Maria Cortez? Dirk's first thought was Maria was most likely Rainer's lover. But he could find no record of Troy travelling down to Mexico City. Why would a man send so much money to a woman he never saw?

Dirk was deep in concentration when he felt a tap on his biceps. He glanced around and found Emory standing behind him with her arms crossed over her chest and a scowl scrunching her beautiful face.

"Tell me, Dirk," Emory leaned forward to read his computer screen over his shoulder. Dirk breathed in her spicy perfume and resisted tugging on the silky curl that tickled his cheek. "Who is Maria Cortez, and what does she have to do with Simeon Gryms? Is she someone who called in with a tip?"

"Not exactly." Dirk minimized his screen.

"I believe I instructed you to work on the Gryms case today, Deputy. It does not make me happy when my orders go unheeded."

Dirk was hyper aware that Hank and Teresa had stopped working and were intently listening to his exchange with their boss. "Emory, come on. You know this case is important to me."

"Perhaps it will help you to remember who's in charge if you call me *Chief*." She glowered at him. "I have not cleared you to work on the Crandall case. The FBI is handling it for now, and you can join the investigation after we find Gryms. Is that clear enough?"

Emory's green eyes flashed with sparks of anger, but her emotion was nothing compared to his. Heat flared in his gut. "Oh, you've Shirley made yourself clear." He used the name Shirley, which he had often teased her with, only this time he implied no joke in his retort. The night they first met at a bar up near his cabin in the Bear Mountains, Emory had told him her name was Shirley. That was before she showed up at work the following Monday as the new Chief Deputy in the Billings US Marshals Office. Once they realized they would be working together, and that she was Dirk's boss, it had been fun to tease her about her fake name. But this time his tone was hard. "But making all four of us focus on a single case is a waste of time, *Chief*."

"If I want your opinion, Deputy, I'll ask for it. For now, get back to work on the Gryms case." She turned on her heel and stalked back to her office.

This was the first time in their relationship that Dirk had been truly angry with Emory. He couldn't believe she pulled rank and called him out in front of Hank and Teresa. Sure, she was the chief of the office, but he had far more experience in the field, and it pissed him off that she refused to listen to him on this.

Teresa stared at Dirk, and he glared at her in return. "What?"

"Nothing!" She raised her hands as if in surrender. "Don't take it out on me. I warned you." Teresa went back to work while Dirk fumed in his chair.

He sent his research and pertinent links to the documents he needed to his personal e-mail. Then he closed the open tabs and resumed listening to messages from women all over the western United States claiming to have seen Simeon Gryms.

Three torturous hours later, it was finally time to call it a day. Dirk pulled on his leather jacket and rattled his car keys. "That's it for me today. I'm out."

Hank glanced at his watch and sighed. Raising her hand in a motionless wave, Teresa's arched brows communicated a vague disapproval, which he shook off. He didn't care what she thought of him leaving early. Emory's door was closed, so he left the office without saying anything to her.

He was waiting for the elevator when Emory strode down the hallway toward him, her heels clattering with purpose.

"Hey, you didn't say goodbye." Her tone was sultry.

Dirk couldn't keep up with her mood changes, and he stared up at the lighted numbers over the doors. "Your office was closed. I didn't want to bother you."

"Will I see you later?" Emory ran her fingers down his arm.

He stiffened. "Not tonight. I have some stuff I need to do."

"Oh," Emory took a step back to study his face. "Is this about earlier? Because that was just work."

The elevator doors opened, and Dirk stepped inside. "I get it. You felt like you had to pull rank on me in front of the others to assert your authority. No big deal. I'll see you tomorrow." He pushed the button for the first floor and met her gaze as the doors closed on her concerned expression.

14

Something was going on between Dirk and the boss, but Teresa didn't want to know. She kept her eye on the clock, planning on leaving at exactly five o'clock. That would get her to Tomas's school early. It was payday, and they would stop by the grocery store on the way home. She had planned their meals and wrote a list that she swore she would not deviate from, no matter how much Tomas begged for some trashy cereal with a prize.

Teresa was waiting by the door with the other parents when the after-school program let out. Tomas continued coloring when the other kids ran to hug their parents. He didn't even look over. The scene was a damning state-ment about the fact she was late, or the last, to pick him up almost every night.

"Tomas?" she called.

His little chin tilted, and he peered up. His face brightened with a huge grin. "Mom! You're here!"

Warmth glowed in her chest at his joy-filled face,

while simultaneously her gut wrenched with guilt at the surprise in his eyes. Her son ran to her and hugged her thighs.

"Hey, don't you need to put away your coloring things?"

"Yeah. Be right back." Tomas dashed back to his coloring pages at the table. He stacked the color book on a pile of others and tossed the crayons he used into the bin.

"Don't forget your backpack."

He zipped to the side of the room where the cubbies stood and grabbed his coat and pack. At seven, Tomas often was too embarrassed to hold his mom's hand, but not that night. He latched onto her hand and pulled her toward the car. All this excitement simply because she was on time. The thought made her nauseous.

After the grocery store, they stopped by the library. Free entertainment was the only kind they had these days. Teresa let Tomas choose two books and two movies. Together, they carried the bags of groceries and the canvas library tote into their house. Tomas practiced his reading while she prepared dinner, but only after he made her promise to let him watch one movie after they ate.

Teresa cooked up a cheesy tuna casserole and served it with canned green beans. She had hoped to have left-overs for another night, but Tomas wanted two large helpings. He must be growing—again. She prayed he wouldn't outgrow his jeans before spring—or worse, his shoes.

After they cleaned up, Tomas changed into his PJs

and sat on the carpet before the TV. While he waited for her to turn on the movie, he played with a small orange truck and a plastic dinosaur she'd never seen before.

"Where did you get those toys?"

Tomas pretended to crunch the truck under T-Rex's enormous feet. "Ms. Frieza."

"Oh? I didn't see her in the after-school room today."

"She wasn't there."

"Did you have art for specials today?"

"No."

"When did you see her, then?"

"At lunch."

"Did she have toys for just you?"

"Yeah."

The random gift seemed odd to Teresa. Why would the teacher single out Tomas? "What for?"

Tomas gave her a quizzical look and shrugged. "'Cuz she's nice?"

Hardened criminals had nothing on little boys. Trying to get information out of him was like shaking the last teaspoon of ketchup out of a jar.

"What did she say when she gave you the toys?"

Tomas rolled his eyes and threw himself backward onto the floor. "She just said she wanted me to have them. Can we watch the movie now?"

Teresa sighed and set up the most recent *Space Jam* movie. She was probably over thinking the whole thing. The woman was only being nice, and if the gift smacked of pity and judgement, so be it. Tomas didn't see it that way. He simply liked the toys.

She stretched out on the sofa and rested her head on

the arm to watch the show, but she drifted off to the opening theme music. The next thing she knew, Tomas was tapping her cheek, and the credits were rolling.

"Wake up, Mom. It's time for bed."

After school the next day, Tomas had another new toy. "Does she give toys to other kids?"

Tomas shrugged. "I don't know."

Teresa pulled on the issue like a loose thread. She couldn't leave it alone. "Do you have to do anything to earn the toys?"

"Not really." Tomas stuffed the new Hot Wheels car into his pack.

"What do you mean by not really?"

"She asked me to take some letter to another teacher, but I didn't do it to get the car. She just gave it to me."

"A letter?"

"Mom," his face scrunched together. "Don't you like it when she gives me toys?"

No. She didn't. "I think you should do nice things for people without expecting a reward. How about no more toys? Okay? If you want toys, ask grandma."

15

———————

As soon as Dirk got home, he unbuttoned his shirt and changed into his favorite comfortable jeans. He trod barefoot to the kitchen, where he poured himself a full glass of red wine and started cooking his dinner. He sauteed onions in butter with garlic. His stomach growled as he breathed in the delectable scent and poured a splash of wine into the mix from his glass. He topped a grilled tri-tip with the onions and served the meat over rice pilaf with slivered almonds. When his roasted veggies were tender, he added them to his plate, and turning on the news, he lounged on the couch to watch. He washed down the over-dramatization and distortion of facts with the full-bodied Cab.

Along the bottom of the TV screen scrolled their most recent image of Simeon Gryms along with the plea for anyone who had seen him to call the posted number with the information. Dirk groaned inwardly. Every time they made the request public, it meant having to sift through hundreds of more calls. He didn't want to think about the Gryms case, though he had to acknowledge that out of the several hundreds of calls a majority of them pointed to Gryms hiding out somewhere in South Dakota.

After Dirk finished his supper, he turned off the TV, switched to his Spotify app for some soothing jazz, and opened his laptop. He reviewed the research he had done earlier that day and concluded that Maria Cortez was at the crux of his investigation into Beaux Crandall's whereabouts. If the woman was so important to Troy, she might know where Beaux was. So far, she was his only lead.

Dirk sifted through hundreds of listings for people named Maria Cortez in Mexico City. There were a surprising number of bed and breakfasts under the name. He searched through criminal records, social media accounts, and personal contact information, reconciling what he found with the banking data he already compiled. Eventually, he narrowed down his list to twenty-four possible Maria Cortezs.

It was almost 9:00 pm when he made his first call asking for Maria and with wobbly Spanish, inquired if the woman knew Troy Rainer. He explained he was looking for beneficiaries of Troy Rainer's estate. Twenty out of twenty-four women stated they didn't know any Troy Rainer. The other four claimed they did, but when questioned further, only one knew where Rainer was when he died and that law enforcement officers killed him. With this one woman, Dirk found the Maria he was looking for.

"I'm sorry for your loss, Ms. Cortez. Would you mind describing your relationship with the deceased?"

"I am his mother," she said in English.

Relieved, Dirk asked, "You speak English?"

"I lived in America for many years."

Dirk's blood fizzed with the excitement of the hunt. "I didn't realize you were Troy's mother since you have different surnames. I thought perhaps you were..."

"Rainer was Troy's father's name. He—I—we were not married."

"I see. Is Mr. Rainer senior an American?"

"Yes."

"Could you please provide me with his phone number? He might also be an inheritor of Mr. Rainer's estate."

"I don't have it. But I'm certain Troy wouldn't have included him in his will. His father abandoned him when he was small. There was bad blood there."

"I see. So, you raised Troy on your own?"

Maria hesitated. "No. I didn't get the chance. Troy's father handed me over to the authorities at the border and they forced me to return to Mexico shortly after Troy was born. I never saw him again. He kept Troy from me. I don't know what happened, but I imagine that having a half Mexican child wasn't as ideal as he originally thought it might be. So, he deserted my boy, and Troy grew up in foster homes. Troy told me he searched and searched until one day he found me, and we reconnected. He was planning to come to Mexico to meet me, but he died before he could."

Dirk softened his voice, rounding it with sympathy. "How did you find out about your son's death?"

"Troy's best friend called me. He told me the police

killed Troy. Hearing that Troy was involved in crime broke my heart. His friend now helps me when he can."

"Helps you, how?"

"He sends me photos of Troy along with a little money, now and then."

Dirk stood and paced to ease the energy crackling in his chest. "Perhaps I should call this friend regarding the money left in Troy's account. It's possible your son mentioned this friend in his will, too."

"I don't have his number, but I could pass on a message for you next time he calls me."

"Actually, I'd rather speak to him in person. What is his name?"

"Beaux Crandall. He and Troy grew up together as foster children. I suppose that's how they got started with their illegal activities. Beaux is American, but I don't think he lives there anymore."

"Do you know where he is now?" Dirk held his breath.

"I think he's been wandering since Troy's death. He said he would send for me when he got settled. Troy had been supporting me for the past several years, you see, and since his death, it has been difficult for me to make ends meet."

"And Crandall has stepped in?"

"Yes, sometimes."

"I see." Dirk's mind raced. He had to keep Maria from telling Crandall that someone called asking questions about him. If she told him, Crandall would disappear again. "Ms. Cortez, I'd prefer to speak to Mr. Crandall myself, if you don't mind. These can be delicate issues. In fact, before we disperse any funds to you, I'd like to meet you in person as well. I would be happy to come down to Mexico City at a convenient time for you."

"Thank you. Any time is fine with me. My days are empty."

"How does Saturday sound?"

Maria gave him her address, surprising Dirk with how trusting she was over the phone with a man she'd never met. This was how people got taken advantage of. As soon as he ended the call with her, Dirk booked a flight early Saturday morning to Mexico City. He would go on his own time and his own dime, avoiding having to ask permission from Emory.

Dirk needed information he didn't have access to, so his next call was to his contact in Interpol. "Marco, it's Dirk. Can you look into some international banking transfers deposited in an account in Mexico City?"

"Does this have to do with the Beaux Crandall case?"

"It does. I think he's been sending money to his deceased friend's mother." Dirk gave Marco the name of the Mexican bank and the account number.

"I'll see what I can do."

"Call me back if you find anything."

"I will. Hey, Sterling. Is this request on the up and up? Why isn't it coming through official channels?"

Dirk swallowed hard. "Crandall is an international criminal. I've been hunting him since his escape from federal custody months ago."

"Which doesn't answer my question."

"It's above board. It's just not officially from my office.

My boss is dragging her heels on this one, but I've got a hot lead I don't want to lose."

Marco sighed. "I'll see what I can find. But keep my name out of it. Will you?"

"Done. I owe you one."

"You do." Humor warmed Marco's tone. "And don't worry, I know where you live."

16

____

Emory looked out the conference room window as she waited for her team to join her for their morning briefing. An overcast steel-gray sky warned of the winter to come. The meeting room door opened, and she turned to see Henry and Teresa enter. They took seats along the side of the long, polished table and prepared the case notes for their requested reports.

"Is Dirk here yet?" Emory didn't like the way they had left things the evening before. She had chastised him in front of the others, and it made him angry. But she had to rein him in. Didn't she? He regularly went off on his own, doing his own thing. He was too much of a maverick, and that wasn't acceptable. She had to maintain the disciplinary structure in the office, or she would lose credibility with the rest of the team.

"Don't worry. I'm not playing hooky," he commented as he entered the room and sat at the head of the table.

Emory smirked to herself at his natural sense of position. "Good morning, everyone. Thank you for preparing for this meeting. I'd like to begin with my findings on the Simeon Gryms case. I've been tracking all the reported sightings since we posted the phone number on the news. We have over seven hundred and fifty calls, and as we know, most of which have been unhelpful, if not entirely untrue. However, I tracked the locations anyway. In the process of doing this, I've seen a pattern that indicates Gryms travelling north from Cheyenne into Montana. From there, it appears he has traveled east into North Dakota. And there have been several reports of people seeing him in cities along I-94. The dates of the sightings coincide with a probable course of travel. It's reasonable to assume that Gryms is hiding out in North Dakota. We don't know whether he'll try to find an unsuspecting woman to support him there, but I think that's a valid assumption. Today, I'd like us to compile a list of wealthy single women in the cities along the interstate. Teresa, why don't you start with Bismarck, and Henry, will you focus on Fargo?'

"No problem, Chief." Teresa reached for her iPad. "I did a similar search to yours." She opened the report she was looking for and turned her device to face the others. "I've only been tracking the phone calls I took, but they seem to show a parallel pattern to the one you found." I've plotted those locations on the map." Teresa swiped to a map of the western United States. Red dots showed the probable places where Gryms traveled. "I thought today I would call back some people who gave more reliable reports of seeing Gryms along this trail and find out if there is any more information I can glean from them."

Emory nodded. "Good, Teresa. Run with that." Teresa

appeared exhausted. Dark circles had formed under her eyes and her cheeks looked hollow. She made a mental note to check in with her admin and then shifted her gaze to Henry.

Her youngest deputy shrugged and stared at the papers spread on the table before him. "I saw nothing different from what you two have found. Searching in North Dakota seems to be the best course of action. I'll start with Fargo, but I don't think it will take long to compile the list, so I can research Bismarck too, if Teresa is still making calls."

"Excellent," Emory smiled, hoping to encourage Henry. He seemed so down. She could tell there was something on his mind but didn't want to pry. As far as she knew, things weren't going well for him at home, but it really wasn't any of her business. "Dirk, what have you discovered?"

Dirk leaned back in his chair and gave her the sexy half grin she found irresistible. "To be honest, Chief, as you know, I haven't really been focusing on this case. However, you'll be happy to hear that in my personal time, I learned some interesting information regarding Beaux Crandall." He held up both hands as if to stop Emory from saying anything. "I know, I know. You ordered me not to work on that case, but I did it on my time off. So, I figured I could get away with that, at least."

The man was beyond aggravating. Emory planned to discuss his blatant insubordination the next time they were alone. If this continued, she wasn't sure their personal relationship would survive.

Dirk leaned forward and braced his forearms on the

edge of the table, waiting until everyone in the room met his eye. "I searched through Crandall's background and found that he and his bodyguard, Troy Rainer, had grown up together in the foster care system in Louisiana. I tracked the time they spent in the foster system and into adulthood. It's occurred to me they were not only employer and employee, but were close friends, as well. Unfortunately, Rainer was a casualty of the raid at the private airport north of Edgar."

He tossed copies of a spreadsheet to each person at the table. "I did a deep dive into Rainer's bank accounts. All the transactions were straightforward except for a monthly electronic transfer sent to a bank in Mexico City. The Mexican account belongs to a woman named Maria Cortez. So, I searched for all the Maria Cortezs in Mexico City, and there were a ton. I pretended to be a banker calling about Rainer's estate and called everyone on the list until I found a woman who not only claimed to know Troy Rainer, but also knew some details of his death.

"I know we use this tactic a lot, but it's always shocking how open people can be with their personal information over the phone. Anyway, Ms. Cortez explained she was Troy's mother, and that they had been separated just after his birth. Apparently, the father turned Maria over to the border patrol and they forced her to return to Mexico. She never saw her son again after that. It seems that Troy found her, though, and had been sending her money for the past couple of years. Maria told me he made plans to travel to Mexico City to meet her, but he died before he had the chance."

Excitement radiated from Dirk's dark eyes, making

them appear almost black. "Now, here's the greatest part. Apparently, Troy's best friend," he made air quotes above his head with his fingers, "has been sending Maria money and a few photos of Troy ever since his death. She's in contact with Crandall, but doesn't know where he is. The mail comes from somewhere outside of the United States. I did my best to convince her not to talk to him about my phone call. I explained I would prefer to speak to him personally since he might also be a recipient of some funds from Troy's estate. She promised not to say anything to him and agreed to allow me to visit her in Mexico City this weekend."

Dirk shot Emory a smug look. "All of this was on my own time, boss. I even booked and paid for my plane ticket. You can't object to that."

A cold lump formed in Emory's belly. She hadn't meant for Dirk to work on his time off or at his personal expense. But she was eager to find Simeon Gryms and bring him in. His was a high-profile case and, as a current news event, would be a boon to her career. She realized now that Dirk was equally determined to hunt down Beaux Crandall, regardless of her priorities, and his motives were more honorable.

"Dirk, I never intended for you to do this work on your own time and certainly not using your own money, but you can't go to another country in an official capacity without approval."

"Of course not." His eyes hardened. "Your intention was that I didn't do it at all. But I can't let this case go. Look, Chief, Crandall is abusing innocent children out there somewhere. To me, that's far more important than finding Gryms who takes advantage of naïve, lonely women. I get that he also shot a guy, so don't get me wrong, I want to find him too, but the two cases just don't compare in importance."

"I understand your point, Dirk, but the caseload isn't for you to decide. We should have spoken about this in my office yesterday. It's my fault we didn't, and I apologize for that. And based on your report, you have my approval to work on this case and to turn in your expenses for the Mexico trip. But I'd like Henry to accompany you." Emory held Dirk's gaze, hoping to negotiate an unspoken peace between them.

Henry looked up from his papers, first at her and then at Dirk. "I want to go to Mexico City with you this weekend. If there's any possibility of catching Crandall, I'm in."

Faced with the team's desire to find Crandall, Emory wondered at her own stubbornness about focusing on Gryms. Maybe she was over-thinking her relationship with Dirk at work. He was right, after all. With the leads he had discovered, they had a solid chance of capturing Crandall and making the world a safer place.

Dirk rolled his chair back and spoke to Henry. "Sure, kid. If you can get a kitchen pass, I'd be glad to have your company. Hopefully, we can convince Maria Cortez that Crandall is the enemy, and that it was his fault that Troy fell into a life of crime in the first place and consequently got shot by the authorities. If she can see Crandall for the disgusting monster he is, we might enlist her help to reel him in."

Emory sat on the edge of the table. "How could Ms.

Cortez assist us if she doesn't know where Crandall is? I doubt he'll tell her."

"She mentioned Crandall wanted to visit her. If she invites him, we will know a date and time to expect him in Mexico City and could coordinate with the Mexican Federales to capture him there. We could then extradite him from Mexico back to the United States to face his original prison sentence along with the additional years he'll have added for his escape."

Dirk's gaze swung to Emory, and he pierced her with a liquid-silver intensity. "Then I will take him to prison myself. He won't get away again."

17

On the way home from work, Hank stopped by the grocery store to pick up Amy's favorite flavor of ice cream. He hoped the surprise would cheer her up. She was in tears again when he left for the office that morning. Sometimes he wondered if they were going to make it through this pregnancy. Hank loved Amy, and he would do anything to help her feel better. But it seemed like everything he tried only made matters worse. The only thing she wanted, that he was not willing to do, was for him to give up his career.

It wasn't just that he had his dream job, or that he had worked so hard to get there. But also, it was the one way he knew he could provide for his family—for the tiny new life they were bringing into the world. Amy didn't understand the pressure he felt to protect them and make certain they had all they needed.

In the freezer section, Hank found Amy's favorite brand of butter pecan. On the way to the checkout, he picked a bouquet of bright yellow and pink blooms to round out his gift. The flowers he brought the day before ended up in the trash. He hadn't seen his wife smile in a long time, and he hoped this combo would do the trick.

Hank struggled to unlock the door, juggling his keys with the ice cream and daisies. He entered the apartment and found Amy sitting at the end of the coffee table in the living room. Next to her stood two pieces of luggage. Her eyes were red as though she had been crying, and if he needed any more proof, the skin on her face was blotchy with angry spots.

"Amy, what's going on? Are you okay? Why do you have your suitcases out?"

"I'm going to stay with my mother for a while. I need some space, and I think this is what's best."

Hank stared at his wife, trying to make sense of what she was saying. "I don't understand." He crossed the room to offer her the bouquet. "I brought home your favorite ice cream. I can scoop you up some. Maybe we could talk while we eat it? How does that sound? I'm sure we can work out whatever this is." Hank swallowed, hoping to rid his words of the desperation that strained his voice.

Amy took the flowers without looking at them and set them on the table next to her. "I don't think ice cream is going to solve our problems. Do you?"

"No, of course not. I just thought it would be a treat for you. But obviously we need to talk. I'm not really sure what our problem is. I mean, I know you don't like my job, but what is so bad you believe we need time apart?" Hank put the ice cream into the freezer and then pulled a chair from the dining table around so that he could sit facing his wife. "Why do you think going to your mother's will help whatever's going on? Shouldn't we work it out together?"

"I can't believe you're acting like you don't know what's wrong." Amy glared at him.

"Well, I know you don't like it when I travel, or when I'm in dangerous situations, but today I was just at the office. Perfectly safe. In fact, I left a little early today. The only reason I didn't get home sooner was because I stopped at the store to get you some things I thought you would like."

Amy crossed her arms over her chest and sighed. "It was a nice thought. And thank you. But ice cream and flowers will not fix what's broken between us. You haven't even considered doing something else for a living. I can see you're not willing to work on this. You don't care how I feel."

Hank braced his elbows on his knees and buried his face in his hands. He swallowed the angry words that wanted to fly and took a deep breath. "Amy, I've worked hard to get where I am in my career, and I don't think it's fair of you to ask me to do something I don't want to do with my life. I can try to travel less. I will tell the chief that I want to stay home with my family more. She makes exceptions for Teresa since she's a single mom, and she might for me too. I'm willing to try those things, but how are you trying to make things better? It seems like there should be some compromise on your side as well. Don't you agree?"

"I will not compromise on what I believe is best for our child. And you having a job where you're home every night and safe, not chasing dangerous criminals who could kill you on any given day, is what's best for our family." Amy rose to her feet and reached for the luggage.

Hank jumped up to stop her. "Listen, I think maybe we should try going to a marriage counselor. An outside perspective might help us come up with ways to work through this issue. What do you think?"

"There's only one solution here, Hank. And clearly, you're not willing to make that change. I don't see how a therapist can help with that. For now, I think we just need a few days apart. I packed everything I could think of that I might need, but I'll call you tomorrow if I realize I've forgotten anything." Amy pulled the handle up on her wheeled luggage, and Hank rested his hand on top of hers.

"Listen, if you insist we take some time apart, I think you should be the one to stay here. Everything you need is here. I'll go. Just give me a few minutes to pack some clothes in a bag."

Amy shrugged and turned away from him, so he reseated the handle and carried her luggage to their bedroom. His stomach hurt, and he felt like he was going to throw up. He'd had such hope when he left work today, and now he had to pack and leave home. Everything was falling apart, and no matter how hard he tried to keep it together, his life was crashing to the ground.

Hank grabbed his gym bag from the closet and stuffed it with enough work shirts to get through the rest of the week, some workout clothes, and a few toiletries. He was certain he was forgetting a lot of things, but he could pick whatever he needed up at the store later.

Amy stood facing out the glass doors to their balcony when he came out of their bedroom.

Hank looped the strap of his bag over his shoulder. "How long do you want me to stay away?"

"I'm not sure." She answered with her back to him.

"Can you help me understand how being apart full time is better than my occasional traveling? I truly don't get it." Desperation clawed at Hank's throat. Maybe they could work this out before he left.

Amy remained silent for a long moment before she said, "I'll worry less if I'm not aware that you're running all over the country chasing murderers. We need to try this separation on for size."

"For size? Are you saying you want to separate forever? Do you want a divorce?"

"I don't know, Hank. I need some time. I'll call you in a few days."

Hank's head spun like it would if a prizefighter had punched him in the face. He glanced around, wondering if this was the last time he would call this apartment home. His chest and throat ached with uncertainty, not knowing if he was supposed to kiss Amy goodbye, or just leave. In the end, he crossed the room, but when Amy did not turn, he touched her shoulders and kissed the back of her head.

"For the record, I don't think this is a good idea. I don't want to be separated and I absolutely do not want a divorce. But I do want to honor your request for some space." With that, Hank left their apartment. He tossed his bag on the seat and sat, not moving, in the cab of his truck. He had no idea where to go.

18

Laurie bought a new violet dress for her date with Dave. She liked how the lines accented her figure. The form-fitting style was decidedly feminine, with its flirty skirt that flared at the hem. She hadn't worn high heels in so long her ankles wobbled. To be safe, she practiced wearing them around the house all afternoon.

While she dressed and primped, Caleb played blocks in the living room under the watchful eye of Bear. When the babysitter arrived, Laurie hurried to answer the doorbell.

"Hi Jenny. Thank you so much for coming tonight."

The teenage girl from next door spoke around a wad of chewing gum. "No problem. I was just hanging out, anyway. May as well hang out with the coolest kid in town. Hey, Caleb."

Caleb jumped up from the floor and ran to throw his little arms around the teen's waist. "Hi Jenny, wanna play blocks?" He didn't wait for her to answer. Instead, he spun around and dove back onto the carpeted floor.

Jenny giggled. "You bet. I'll be right there. Any special instructions for tonight?" she asked Laurie.

"Dinner is in the refrigerator. You just need to heat it in the microwave. I told Caleb you guys could have popcorn with a movie before bed. I'm sure he'll hold you to that." Laurie smiled fondly at her son and his dog lying side by side on the floor. "We shouldn't be late. It's just dinner."

Jenny grinned. "You are rocking that dress. Hot date?"

Laurie's cheeks heated. "I guess so." She let out a soft laugh. "I'm going to go finish getting ready. If my date gets here before I come back out, give me a holler."

"No problem." Jenny sat next to Caleb and added a block to his tower.

Laurie returned to her bathroom to put the finishing touches on her hair. It had grown so long since she's last had it cut. It must have been before Sam died. She hadn't been great about taking care of herself after she lost her husband. A wave of sadness washed through her, and she didn't resist it. She had learned that the waves of sudden grief were temporary. Laurie focused on the moment and her date for the night. She was really looking forward to having an adult evening out with a new man, and David seemed to like Caleb when they had met before. That was always a good sign.

The doorbell rang, and a clump of nerves burst into sparklers in Laurie's belly. Quickly, she applied lipstick and gloss. She walked through a spray of floral perfume, popped her lips, and patted her hair before hurrying out to greet Dave.

He gave a low whistle when he saw her. "You're gorgeous." His eyes gleamed with appreciation.

Laurie smoothed the skirt of her dress with trembling fingers. "Thank you. You look very handsome tonight, too." Dave straightened the navy sports coat he wore over an open-collared shirt and dark blue jeans. "Caleb, come and say hello to Dave."

Her son made no move to stand. "Hi." He waved without looking at her date. Embarrassed, Laurie shrugged with a what-can-you-do expression. "Boys and their blocks."

Dave gave her an understanding smile. "Hey, buddy. What are you building there?"

"An outer space castle."

Dave took two steps into the living room to see the structure but stopped abruptly when Bear emitted a low growl.

"Bear, no!" Laurie's cheeks flamed at their dog's reaction to Dave. "He's actually a friendly dog. I promise."

"He's just being protective of his boy." Dave turned and touched her elbow. "Ready to go?"

He took her to a surf-and-turf restaurant where he ordered for them both. Laurie would have preferred the grilled salmon, but since he didn't ask, she decided she would also appreciate the steak. He requested a bottle of Cabernet for the table and stuffed mushrooms to start with. Over the appetizer, Dave asked about her day.

"To be perfectly honest..." Laurie smiled and looked

down at her hands clenched together in her lap. "I spent the whole day shopping for this dress and getting ready for our date. I suppose I shouldn't admit that to you."

"Time well spent from where I sit. You are beautiful, and I love the dress." Dave popped a mushroom into his mouth and took his time chewing. He studied her during a long swallow of wine. "So, have you seen much of Dirk lately?"

The question surprised her but gave her something they had in common to talk about. "Yes, in fact, he comes over once a week for dinner. I think he feels obligated to be there for Caleb ever since we lost Sam. And I must admit, it's nice to have him around."

"I get that. What's he working on these days?" Dave chomped on another mushroom.

"He talked a little about hunting for the guy who shot the armored car guard down in Denver. Did you hear about that on the news?"

Dave wiped his mouth with his napkin. "Yeah, I think I remember hearing something about that. So, Sterling's not pursuing Beaux Crandall anymore?"

Why was Dave making Dirk the topic of conversation. Maybe he was nervous, too. "Honestly, I don't really know what Dirk is doing at work. He didn't say anything to me, but then again, why would he?"

"No reason, I guess. I just thought you two were close."

"We are. But mostly we chat about Caleb and life." Laurie didn't mention that Dirk didn't like the fact that Dave wanted to date her. She didn't figure that little tidbit would go over very well.

"Have you seen Emory lately?"

Ah, so this was where he was going with the conversation the whole time. Emory. Dave had been in love with Emory for several months. They dated, but she ended up choosing Dirk over him. "I haven't spoken to Emory in weeks. I know she and Dirk are seeing each other, but he doesn't really talk much about that, either. He's a pretty private guy."

"Well, good for them."

Laurie raised an eyebrow.

Laughing, he said, "No, I mean it. I know she's had feelings for him for a long time. It would have never worked out between us, anyway. And besides, now I get to sit here across the table from you." He lifted his glass in a silent toast to her.

After they had finished their meals, the waiter returned to see if they wanted dessert. Dave ordered a chocolate torte to share. "And coffee, please."

Laurie spoke up. "Actually, I'd prefer tea. If you don't mind." The waiter nodded and left for the kitchen.

"I'm sorry, I just assumed." Dave reached across the table and took her hand.

She liked the feel of her hand in his much larger one. She couldn't remember the last evening she spent with a man who was interested in her, since Sam. At one point, she had hoped that something would develop between her and Dirk, but she was even more grateful for his friendship.

Laurie pressed Dave's fingers with her own. "That's alright. I just tend to drink tea in the evenings rather than coffee. Too much caffeine keeps me up at night."

A spark ignited in Dave's eyes. "That could be a good thing." His mouth curved into a suggestive smile.

A jolt of sexually charged electricity zipped through Laurie's blood. She thought about what might happen later. She couldn't invite Dave in after the first date, could she? Well, if she counted the coffee as a date, this was technically the second one. She smiled and bit down on her lower lip.

When he drove her home, Dave parked at the curb outside her house. He got out, rounded the hood, and opened her door. Holding out his hand, he helped her out of the car and wove his fingers with hers as he walked her to the door. "I had a great time tonight, Laurie."

"Yes, so did I." A sudden shyness overcame her. "Thank you for dinner."

Dave stopped with her on the porch. He touched her chin and looked deep into her eyes. He tilted her face up and bent to kiss her goodnight. When his lips met hers, Laurie slid her arms around him and welcomed his kiss.

When they broke apart, Dave's breath came fast. "Do you want me to take your babysitter home?"

Laurie blinked opened her eyes. "No thanks, that's not necessary. Jenny lives next door." She stared into his eyes, and the words flowed. "Would you like to come in?"

"Absolutely." Dave drew her close and kissed her again.

The front door swung open, and they jumped apart, startled to see Dirk glowering at them through the screen. "Good to see you got home safe and sound, Laurie. It's a bit after the pumpkin hour." He chuckled, but the sound held no warmth.

"Dirk!" Laurie was stunned. "What are you doing here?"

"I stopped by to visit Caleb and decided to hang out with him for the rest of the evening, so I sent Jenny home. Hope that's okay." His steely gray gaze moved from her to Dave, and his expression hardened. "Aldrich."

Dave straightened and tugged on his jacket. "Sterling. Good to see you. How's work?"

"Same old, same old."

"Any luck in finding Crandall?"

"Maybe. I'm trying, but the boss keeps me working on another case."

"It's an FBI hunt, anyway. Emory understands that."

Dirk didn't respond to that comment. Laurie pulled opened the screen door. Dave took her hand and followed her inside. Instead of leaving, Dirk resumed his seat on the couch in front of the TV and made no move to give them any privacy.

"I appreciate you watching Caleb, Dirk. But it's getting late. Are you planning on staying?" Laurie's voice wavered on the question. She wasn't certain how to handle the situation, but she wanted Dirk to go so that Dave could stay.

Dirk smirked. "Just until the end of my movie. You don't mind, do you?"

Laurie looked helplessly at Dave. He shook his head. "Goodnight, Laurie. I hope we can do this again soon."

She walked him to the door, where they shared a last kiss. When she returned to the living room, she parked her hands on her hips. "Seriously, Dirk? I can't believe you. Can't you take a hint?"

"Oh, I got the hint alright. But this is your first date with him, Laurie. And I don't know if I trust Aldrich that much. I think you should take things slow."

"And *I* think the speed of my relationship is none of your business."

19

____

Later, when Dirk got home, Emory was waiting for him on his front deck. She sat in the glow of the lanterns she had lit next to the porch swing. As he mounted the steps, he noticed she had bundled herself up in one of the blankets he kept outside in a trunk for that purpose.

Warily, he stopped at the top stair. "I didn't expect to see you here tonight. Is everything alright?"

"I'm fine. I hope this is a pleasant surprise." Emory swung her legs off the swing to make room for him, but he remained standing.

"Yes, of course it is. How long have you been here?"

"Since about 7:30. I read until it got too dark, then I lit your lanterns. You don't mind, do you? I really should have called first." The candlelight gleamed in her green eyes and cast a beautiful glow across her skin.

"You can come here whenever you want. Sorry I was so late. I was babysitting Caleb. Did you know Dave Aldrich took Laurie out for dinner tonight?"

Emory bit down on her lip as she studied him. "No. How do you feel about that?"

Dirk joined her on the swing. "Honestly, I don't like it. But probably not for the reasons you think. I don't have those kinds of feelings for Laurie, but there's something about Aldrich that just doesn't sit right with me."

"But you still babysat?"

"I stopped by, and when I found out Laurie was out, I sent her sitter home and hung out with the little guy."

"Did Laurie have a nice time?" Emory slid her hand into his.

Dirk shrugged. "I suppose so. I'm pretty sure Aldrich intended to spend the night. Good thing I was there."

Emory let out a soft laugh. "Why was that a good thing? Laurie is an adult. She's fully capable of making her own decisions."

"Yeah, but it was only their first date."

This time, Emory laughed out loud. "Dirk, you're not her father. Laurie is a beautiful and intelligent woman who can make up her own mind about her personal life. You need to stay out of it."

Dirk's mouth quirked into a reluctant grin. "I suppose you're right. I just feel protective of them." He draped his arm over Emory's shoulders and drew her close. "Besides, I have my own personal life to work on." He pressed his lips against her temple and trailed kisses down her cheekbone until he found her lips.

The heat of their passion flared, and Emory broke away to whisper, "Let's go inside."

Dirk stood and helped Emory to her feet. He unlocked the front door, and the two of them left a trail of clothing from there to his bedroom. Taking her hand, he led her into the bathroom, where he turned on the shower.

As the stream of warm water flowed over them, Dirk asked, "Does this mean you forgive me for ignoring the Gryms case in favor of Crandall?"

"I don't want to talk about work. I think it's best if we keep our personal lives and our professional lives completely separate."

"Sure, in a perfect world. But I don't think that's possible in reality."

Emory slid her fingers into his wet hair and pulled him down for a kiss. "I suppose you're right. So, in that case, I forgive you. Now, let's get back to the personal part of our lives, shall we?"

A loud banging sounded on the periphery of Dirk's awareness. He shrugged it off in favor of passion, but the noise grew more insistent.

"What is that?" Emory's words came in quick breaths.

"Who cares?" Dirk nibbled the graceful column of Emory's neck, but she pulled away.

"It sounds like someone's at the front door. The knocking is urgent, Dirk. I think you better answer it."

Dirk groaned. "Can't we just ignore it?" He reached for her.

She stepped out of his grasp. "No. If someone is banging on your door this late at night, it must be important. Someone might need help. Go see who it is."

Irritation snaked its way up his spine. He was far more interested in reconnecting with Emory. They'd been at odds all week and were finally putting their tension to rest. He didn't really care if his neighbor needed to borrow a cup of sugar. There were other neighbors. Yanking a towel off the rod, he ran it over his wet hair, then wrapped it around his waist. "Don't go anywhere. I'll be right back."

Dirk strode to the door and yanked it open. Before him stood a distraught Hank with a full duffel bag slung over his shoulder, holding a bottle of Buffalo Trace in one hand, and a tub of vanilla ice cream in the other. "Hey, kid. What's going on?"

"Amy says she needs some space. Is there any way I can spend the night on your couch?"

On any other night, Dirk would have flung the door wide open for his partner. But with Emory naked in the shower waiting for him, he hesitated.

"Of course." Emory's silky voice sounded from Dirk's bedroom door. "Come in, Henry."

Dirk spun his head around to see her wrapped in his black terry robe, her wet her hair twisted up in a towel, and disappointment weighed heavily on his shoulders. He cocked his jaw to the side before turning back to Hank. "You heard the woman. Come on in."

"Oh God, I'm sorry. I'll go somewhere else. I..."

Emory marched across the room. She reached for Hank's arm and pulled him into the house. "Absolutely not. You shouldn't be alone tonight. Come in, and I'll get you some tea. But first, excuse me for a minute."

Dirk closed the door behind them and watched Emory, along with his plans for the night, disappear into his bedroom. "Let's open that bourbon before she makes you that god-awful chamomile tea or some shit."

A brief smile cast a shadow over Hank's mouth. "I'm sorry to interrupt, dude. I didn't see the chief's car outside, or I would have just driven past."

"Not a big deal. What happened with Amy? She kicked you out?"

"She says she needs some space. I'm afraid she's trying separation on for size to see if she likes it better than being married. She had her suitcases packed and ready to go to her mother's house when I got home from work tonight. I insisted she stay at the apartment and told her I would leave. Tomorrow, I'll find another place. I think you can rent a room by the week."

"How long does she want you to stay away?"

Hank let his bag slide down his arm and land on the floor at his feet. "I don't know for sure."

"If you want, you can use my spare bedroom as long as you need to." Dirk took the bottle from Hank and poured them each a drink.

"Thanks, but I don't want to intrude." Hank inclined his head toward Dirk's closed bedroom door. "I really am sorry I screwed up your night."

"Don't be. Partners come first. Besides," Dirk gave Hank a wicked grin, "the night's not over yet. Put your stuff in your room, and I'll start a fire."

Hank nodded and passed the tub of ice cream to Dirk.

"What the hell is this? Did you think we'd eat this from the carton while we painted our toenails and braided each other's hair?" Dirk was relieved when a reluctant grin brightened Hank's face.

"Haven't you ever had a bourbon float?"

"No. But why would you wreck a perfectly good whiskey?"

Dirk remembered all he had on was a towel when Emory joined them, fully dressed. She took the frozen dessert from him and put it in the freezer. With a gentle laugh, she said, "It's actually pretty good, but you're missing some ingredients. You make the floats with bourbon cream, which is like Bailey's Irish Cream only made with whiskey, and then you add root beer."

"Gross. I'll keep mine neat, thanks. You girls do what you want. I'm gonna get dressed." When Dirk returned, he lit a fire to take the night's chill off.

They sat together in the quiet living room, listening to the crackling flames. Finally, Hank lifted his glass in a toast. "At least I can fly down to Mexico with you in the morning with no hassles. Apparently, I have nowhere better to be."

20

Dirk and Hank left early the next morning for their flight to Mexico City. When they arrived, they picked up their rental car. Dirk drove while Hank navigated them through the busy city streets.

"Man, that was a hairy landing coming into the airport." Hank commented once they were on the highway.

"Yeah," Dirk agreed. "I thought I was going to lose a few teeth on touchdown."

"It's a pretty sketchy approach in there on a clear day with the altitude and the mountainous terrain but add in the gusty winds and you're glad you have a skilled pilot in the cockpit."

They exited the freeway and made their way into the city center, passing the iconic Art Museum. Dirk slowed so they could look up at the beautiful neoclassical building inspired by ancient Greek and Roman architecture, with its golden domes and palatial columns.

"Look at that building!" Hank's voice was filled with

awe. "I wish we had time for sightseeing while we were here. I'd love to see inside."

Dirk chuffed. "Not me. We're so close to catching Crandall right now I can taste it. That's got my total focus. You should bring Amy back here sometime."

Hank ignored his suggestion. "Have you thought about how much you're going to share with Ms. Cortez when we get there?" Hank studied the GPS map on his phone. "Seems like she might be loyal to Crandall."

"I'll take a read when we meet her, but I plan to be straight up with her. I think that's our best chance to sway her to our side."

Hank pointed out the windshield. "Turn left on the next street."

They made their way to the western edge of the city. After meandering through one suburb after another, they eventually found the little community Maria had described. The GPS map guided them to a row of concrete houses. An older woman sat outside of one with an orange metal sliding door that opened to a small chipped-cement courtyard. There was no sidewalk to speak of, so Dirk parked in front of the opening. They stepped out of the car and approached the woman.

Her hands stilled from stitching bright flowers onto the collar of a blouse. She studied them with dark eyes set in her lined face. She wore her graying hair pulled into a tidy bun at her nape.

Dirk removed his sunglasses. "*Disculpe. Estamos buscando a una mujer llamada María Cortez.*"

She nodded. "Mr. Sterling?"

"Yes, ma'am." Dirk smiled, relieved they could

continue in English due to his limited Spanish. "And this is my partner, Hank Flanigan."

Maria set down her sewing basket and stood. "Please come inside. It's cooler in the house."

Dirk and Hank followed Maria into the home made of cinderblocks and painted the same orange as the gate. Their northern Montana blood was unaccustomed to the blistering heat, and they were thankful to get out of the sun. The thick walls kept the house at a comfortable temperature. She offered them agua fresca, and they gratefully accepted the refreshing fruit-infused drink.

Maria gestured for them to sit at a rustic kitchen table. "You do not look like bankers or lawyers to me."

"No, ma'am. We're not. In truth, we are Deputy US Marshals."

Maria's expression did not change. Surprise never crossed her features. "I didn't figure Troy left much of an estate. Certainly not anything large enough to merit a banker from the US flying all the way down here to visit me."

"You're a perceptive woman, Maria." Dirk leaned forward. "Let me tell you why we're here. You may be unaware, but your son was mixed up in some serious crimes."

"Is that why he got shot? Because of the crime he was involved in?"

"Yes, ma'am. And we're sorry for your loss, Maria. Troy worked as a bodyguard for a man named Beaux Crandall and they were also close friends. My research shows they grew up in the Louisiana foster care system. They spent plenty of time in juvenile hall together before they turned eighteen. I suspect that's where they learned their life of crime."

Maria sighed and pressed her face with her hand. "This is all Troy's father's fault. My son might have had a chance if his father raised him. But instead, he cast the boy aside. The biggest heartbreak of my life was when that *bastardo* separated me from my child for no reason at all."

"Troy certainly would have been better off with you. Unfortunately, he hitched his wagon to Beaux Crandall, who built a criminal empire through importing and selling drugs, gun smuggling, and worst of all, he's made a fortune through human trafficking."

Maria's eyes widened. "My Troy was involved in human trafficking?"

Hank folded his arms on the table. "Yes. Unfortunately, he was. But the instigator of it all was Crandall. And ultimately it was because of your son's involvement with Crandall that he was in the shoot-out where he lost his life."

Dirk sipped his drink to give Maria a moment to process the information. When she raised her saddened eyes to his, he continued. "Crandall was prosecuted and sentenced to life in prison. But on his way to jail, someone ambushed his guards and Crandall escaped. He fled the country and is hiding out on a beach somewhere. You are our only chance to find him and put him behind bars where he belongs."

"I see." Maria sat quietly for several minutes. "Mr. Crandall was Troy's only friend. The only person he was close to. I feel disloyal to my son for even talking to you about Mr. Crandall. I'm sure you can understand."

Dirk set his glass down and scooted his chair closer to Maria. He gazed deeply into her eyes. "I do understand. It's why I was less than honest about who we are when I spoke with you on the phone. We wanted a chance to ask for your help in person. I have some pictures I'd like to show you. They'll help you grasp the kind of man Beaux Crandall really is and the horrible things he does to the innocent women and children he steals off the streets. Their families are left wondering if their loved ones are dead or alive." He lowered his voice. "If they knew what their children were going through, they would probably rather they were dead."

Maria briefly closed her eyes, and pressing her lips together, she drew in a deep breath through her nose. Hank handed Dirk his iPad, and he positioned the screen so Maria could see the damning images. He scrolled through photos taken at Crandall's ranch in Montana and displayed several shots they had pulled off the dark web that the prosecution presented as evidence against Crandall at his trial. But he left out the snuff films featuring Troy. Dirk concluded by showing Maria the faces of each of the children they had rescued during the raid in which her son was killed. As she watched the images on the pad, Maria's face grew pale and her hands trembled.

She closed her eyes, pressing out hovering tears. Blinking open her lids, Maria stared at Dirk. "Who could do something like this to children?" She cried softly.

Dirk understood she wept because she already knew

the answer to her question. "Maria, it was Beaux Crandall who involved your son in these despicable things. He is the monster. But the hard truth is, Troy took part in the abuse and even the murder of innocent victims. Troy paid for his sins with his life, but Crandall is still somewhere out there in the world, free to continue these heinous crimes against innocent children." He paused, and clearing his throat, he opened another file on the iPad. "I have one more thing to show you. This is the last communication we received from Crandall. He sent it to taunt me." Dirk clicked on the video that Crandall sent showing him sitting on a beach being served by a young girl who cried when he fondled her and sneered at the camera with a sickening twisted laugh. Maria covered her face with her hands.

Dirk spoke quietly. "So, you can see why we're desperate to find him. Crandall seems to trust you, Maria. You're our only chance."

He sat back in his chair and waited. Maria stood and paced the small room, worrying the fabric of her blouse. Finally, she turned to face them. "How can I help you? I will do whatever you need me to do."

Dirk gave her a gentle and encouraging smile. "You told me on the phone that Crandall contacts you sporadically. That he has sent you pictures of Troy and money to support you."

"Yes." Maria moved across the room to a cabinet where she located a carved wooden box. She brought it to the table and opened the lid. Her fingers filed through several envelopes until she found the one she looked for, and she drew it out. "This is the last letter I received from Mr. Crandall." She handed it to Dirk, who studied the address and postmark before he unfolded the envelope and slid out the paper inside.

It was a handwritten note from Crandall expressing his grief over the loss of his best friend.

"He sent cash with this letter, too. Other times he's wired money into my account."

Dirk flipped the envelope over and studied the postmark. "This letter came from Morocco." He glanced at Hank. "I pictured him somewhere in the Caribbean. Was the cash in pesos?"

"No. US one-hundred-dollar bills."

Hank read the envelope. "The postmark may or may not mean anything. He could have been traveling or had a friend or associate mail it. But if he is in Morocco, like a number of countries in Africa, they have no extradition agreement with the US."

"True." Dirk returned the letter to Maria. "If you don't mind, I'd like to borrow the correspondence you've received from both your son and Crandall. We can have FBI analysts go over them and see what they find."

"Of course." Maria put the letter back into the box and handed the entire thing to Dirk. "This is all of them. But please return my son's letters to me when you're finished. They are all I have of him... He was my son—even if he did horrible things."

"Of course we will. It might take time because investigators will need the letters for evidence in court, but I'll make certain they get back to you." Dirk's heart wrenched at the sorrow painted across the woman's face. He hated doing this to her. Her situation was tragic. "You mentioned Crandall was hoping to visit you at some point. Is that correct?"

"Yes, but we have made no plans."

Hank took the box of letters from Dirk and nestled them in his bag next to the iPad. He looked up at Maria. "Do you have any way of contacting Crandall? Did he give you his phone number?"

"No, he calls me."

"Would you mind letting us look at your phone bill?"

"Let me get it for you." Maria made her way to a small desk in the corner of the room. She snapped open a plastic file box and pulled out several sheets of paper.

Hank flipped through the stack of invoices. "When did Crandall last contact you?"

"Just last month." Maria watched over his shoulder as he sifted through the papers. She pointed when he found the September bill. "There."

There were only a few recorded calls, and most of them were obviously local.

"This one was an international call." Hank showed the number to Dirk. "Country code +212. That shouldn't be hard to trace." He raised excited eyes.

Dirk gave Hank a nod and then rested a gentle hand on Maria's shoulder. "Maria, may I take these statements along with the letters?"

"Yes, of course. If you think they will help."

Dirk reached for the woman's hands. He clasped them together in his own much larger ones and peered down into her sad face. "I do. You have been more helpful than you know, and I wonder if you'd be willing to do one more thing. Will you help us trap Crandall?"

She blinked up at him. "What do you mean? How can I do that?"

"The next time Crandall calls you, I want you to pretend you recently found out that you're very ill. We will build you a false medical history, one that shows that you're dying of cancer, or something. You can tell him your doctor has given you mere weeks to live, and the one thing you'd like more than anything is to meet your son's best friend. That Crandall is all you have left of Troy." Dirk paused and pressed Maria's fingers. "I'm sorry to use the loss of your son as a ploy, but it's our only option. If we can convince Crandall to come to see you in Mexico, it will make capturing him much easier. He could be anywhere in the world, and he is smart. Smart enough to stay hidden. As far as I can tell, he has only one weakness, and that is the relationship he had with Troy."

Hank reached for his iPad and quietly tapped on the screen. "The country that international code is from is Morocco. Which lends weight to the speculation of him hiding out in that part of the world. Of course, the attached country code doesn't mean it's where the call originated."

"No." Dirk rubbed his jaw. "But it *is* where the phone was registered."

Hank brought up a world map and zoomed in to northwest Africa. "He could have set up shop on one of the beaches along the coast."

"Maybe..."

"Dirk! Check out these islands off the coast!"

"What country do they belong to?"

"The archipelago is a small, independent country

called Cabo Verde." Hank spread his fingers across the screen to enlarge the image. "Any of these beaches could be Crandall's location on the video."

"I've never even heard of Cabo Verde."

"Yeah, you have. It's the country where they extradited that Columbian business executive to the US for money laundering and violating the embargo placed against Iran a couple of years ago."

Dirk drew his brows together. "We have an extradition treaty with them?"

"No. The United States wanted to extradite the man for breaking the law, but the government of Cabo Verde refused to comply. The Columbian remained on the island, knowing as soon as he left, he would get arrested. In the end, the US sent a SEAL team in to abduct him, and he's now awaiting his trial in a Florida jail cell."

"Oh, yeah. I remember that. It was a total shit show. And I can see why Crandall might choose those islands, knowing that he wouldn't face extradition and wouldn't likely get kidnapped either after all the terrible publicity the US received the last time."

Hank settled his gaze on Maria. "So, ma'am, you can see how necessary it is for us to get Crandall to come to Mexico?"

Turning to Maria, Dirk nodded. "If we can get him to visit you, we can arrest him here and take him back to the United States, where he'll face his original charges along with escaping prison and killing the guards. All we need you to do is convince Crandall to come. You don't need to see him or spend any time with him. We'll grab him as soon as he touches down at the airport. Do you think you can do that?"

"I will try. I am sick knowing that my son was involved in any of this. Helping you is the least I can do to make up for him."

After writing out a script for Maria to use the next time Crandall called her, and making sure she had both Dirk's and Hank's personal cell phone numbers, Dirk pulled out his wallet and handed Maria several hundred-dollar bills in cash.

"There's a reward for helping the US Marshals capture Crandall. And you'll receive that money once he's in custody. You can live on those funds for many years to come, but hopefully, this will help in the meantime. We are in your debt."

The men said their goodbyes and returned to their car. On the way back to the airport, Dirk called his contact in Interpol. "Marco, it's Sterling. I think we may have located Crandall. At least we have a general area. Can you look into wealthy Americans living in Cabo Verde? It's a string of islands off the west coast of Africa."

"Yeah." Marco's Italian accent rolled through the phone speaker. "I'll check things out. But you know, you have no legal authority there."

"Don't worry, we've got a plan. See what you can find out, and I'll call you on Monday."

"You got it. But I hate it when you tell me not to worry because you have a plan. Stay safe. Talk soon."

Dirk shoved his phone into his pocket and turned to Hank. "Step on the gas, kid. We have a lot of research to wade through, and even more coordinating to get every-thing in place while we wait for Crandall to call Maria."

21

"How was the trip to Mexico?" Emory was the last to join the morning meeting. She slid into the chair at the head of the table, opposite Dirk at the other end. Henry and Teresa sat in their usual spots on the long side facing the window with their work spread out around them.

"More fruitful than we could have hoped for." Dirk sipped his coffee. "We found Maria Cortez to be very open and helpful. She was quick to see that Crandall was to blame for her son's criminal activity and ultimately his death. She's more than willing to help us trap him."

Emory shifted her gaze from the laptop screen to Dirk's triumphant expression. "Trap him?"

Dirk's mouth slid into one of his irresistible lopsided grins. For a moment her focus rested there, but she quickly snapped her attention back to his words. "Yes. During our trip we learned Crandall sometimes sends Maria money and occasionally calls her. After we showed her evidence of Crandall's treachery, she gave us access to her phone records. We now have a phone number associated with him that originated in Morocco. Unfortunately, there is no way of knowing if that's where he was when he made the call, only that the country code is Moroccan. It's unlikely Crandall is hiding out there, but Hank discovered a tiny country made up of a string of islands called Cabo Verde. It's off the coast of western Africa. My connection in Interpol is poking around there to see if he can find any trace of Crandall."

"Is that part of the Canary Islands?" Teresa stretched over to look at a map on Henry's iPad.

Dirk shook his head. "No. The Canary Islands belong to Spain and would be far more likely to extradite Crandall than Cabo Verde."

Henry tapped on his screen and shared a map of western Africa to the smart board above Dirk's head. "Cabo Verde has no extradition treaty with the United States, and there is bad blood in that regard. You may remember from the news coverage a few years ago, when a Seal Team was deployed to abduct a Columbian businessman named Saab. He was arrested and forcibly taken to the United States to stand trial." He circled the island nation in red on the screen.

"Yes. I remember, but what does that have to do with this case?" Emory studied the map.

Dirk answered, "The US received a black eye in the media for taking the action which makes Cabo Verde a brilliant place to hide. Our government doesn't want to go stir up any more negative international press. "That being the case," he added, "if Crandall is there, we need to get him to leave that country and go to a friendly nation so we can arrest him and bring him back here to face his charges."

Emory bit down on the end of her pen and stared at the map. "But what if he's not in Cabo Verde?"

"It doesn't really matter where he is. If we can trick Crandall into visiting Maria Cortez in Mexico, we can arrest him there and bring him back to the US."

"Okay, then why ask your contact to snoop around there?"

Dirk's eyes hardened, changing their color from stormy gray to flint. "We must rescue Crandall's victims."

Emory admired Dirk's strategic yet empathetic mind. He was excellent at his job and never hesitated to act. Of course, sometimes his bold decisiveness caused problems when he chose to act against her orders. "I agree. So how do you plan to get Crandall to visit Ms. Cortez?"

Henry sat forward, glancing at Dirk for approval. When he got the nod, Henry turned to her with excitement sparkling in his eyes. It was good to see him energized again. The last time she'd seen him at Dirk's house, he'd been sullen and depressed.

"Maria is going to tell Crandall that she's dying of cancer and that her final wish is to meet the man who was her son's best friend. She'll ask him to visit her at her home in Mexico City because she is unable to travel due to her poor health."

Teresa leaned back in her chair bouncing in the reclining seat. "Do you think that'll work? Crandall is wily. Don't you think he'll be suspicious?"

Dirk raised one shoulder. "It's worth a try. Other options could include an abduction. But as we've learned from the past, that doesn't go over very well on the global scene."

Teresa tapped her pen on the edge of the table. "You'd think everyone would want that kind of scum arrested. No matter what country he currently lives in."

"Everyone except the sick bastards who participate in the kind of crime Crandall propagates." Dirk swung his gaze to Emory. "So, what do you think?"

"I agree it's worth a try and seems like our best shot. So now we wait for Maria Cortez to receive a call and set up a time?"

"Yes, and in the meantime, I'm working with Interpol and the Mexican police. Both agencies are poised and ready to assist us along with teams from ATF and ICE when the time comes. Until then, it's a waiting game."

"Aren't you including the FBI?"

"Not at this time."

Emory glanced at the meeting agenda on her laptop screen. "Okay. Keep me posted with any updates.

"Now, let's move on to the Gryms case. We've had a phone call from a Cora Johnson in Bismarck who thinks she might be living with the man we're looking for. Apparently, Ms. Johnson met this man at a local community event. He wined and dined her, and they ended up in a relationship. He moved into her home, and about a week later the woman noticed various valuables were missing. She had heard about Simeon Gryms on the news, but our description did not fit the man she is living with. Our last known images of Gryms show him with long blonde hair and sporting a surfer look.

"The man she is living with calls himself Don Williams, and has short brown hair parted on the side that he keeps precisely trim and neat, and he wears glasses. Williams doesn't look like the man in the photos on TV, but the more she heard about Gryms in the news, the more her situation sounded similar. Ms. Johnson took a picture of the man she's living with and held it side by side to a screen shot of the images of Gryms. When she saw the facial resemblance, she called the number on the news. I have since spoken on the phone with her and find her story credible."

Henry jotted a few last notes before he asked, "So this Williams guy is still living in her home?"

"Yes." Emory carefully avoided looking at Dirk. "And so, I need you and Dirk to fly up to North Dakota and investigate it. If this man is indeed Simeon Gryms, it should be a simple nab and grab scenario. It would be wonderful to put this case to bed." The intensity of Dirk's stare caused her neck to heat, but she swallowed and met his gaze head on.

"Can't you have the local cops investigate?" Dirk leaned back in his chair and crossed his arms over his chest.

"It's too risky. I don't want to take the chance of anything going wrong. When you get there, if you determine the man is Gryms, then I expect you to call for backup from the local police department before attempting to arrest him. He's already shown that he's willing to kill to get away."

In her peripheral view, Henry's head swiveled between her and Dirk as they discussed the day's plan, until finally his gaze settled on her. "When do you want us to leave?"

"I realize you've had to travel a lot recently, Henry. I hope it's not causing any problems for you."

"No, ma'am. Since Amy and I are on a marital break, she doesn't know, or even care, if I'm home."

Emory sent an inquiring look toward Dirk, who shrugged.

"Very well, then, I'd like you to head over to Billings first thing tomorrow morning. Teresa, will you please arrange their travel?"

Teresa scribbled a note on a sticky pad in front of her. "No problem. And the return trip?"

"Leave it open for now."

Dirk sighed angrily. "Are we done here?"

"I realize this is not your first choice, Dirk. But since you're waiting for developments in the Crandall case anyway, I think it's good timing."

Dirk's phone buzzed. He glanced at the screen and sent a questioning gaze to Emory. She nodded, and he answered the call. "Sterling here." He listened to the caller, occasionally nodding, and making affirmative noises. "Sounds like you did an excellent job, Maria. Next time he calls, tell him you really want to see him before it's too late. As soon as you set a date for his visit, let me know." When Dirk ended the call, his dark eyes bore into hers. "Whatever date Maria sets with Crandall will become my top priority. No matter what other case you have me on. Just so you know."

"I'm still the one who makes those determinations in this office, Deputy Sterling." Emory met his harsh gaze with one of her own. "This meeting is over. Sterling, I'd like to see you in my office." She closed her laptop and carried it with a purposeful stride out the door.

Dirk followed her into her office and closed the door behind him. She turned to face him, anger fortifying her courage. "I thought we came to an understanding You cannot challenge my authority in front of the others. It's hard enough having them know we're in a relationship, without you trying to ram-rod your decisions through in an attempt to supersede mine. The orders I give on this team are what goes. Do you understand?"

Dirk stared her down, but something shifted in the depths of his eyes. He stretched his hand toward her, slipping his fingers around to the back of her neck. He pulled her into him tilting her chin up with his other hand. Frustrated by his lack of decorum—and basic insubordination—she pushed against his chest.

"It turns me on when you're so commanding." Smoky humor glinted in his eyes as he bent to kiss her.

Her mind fought to resist him, but her body ignored her brain. By the time she managed to pull back they were both breathing heavily, and she was furious. She wanted to smack the insolent smirk off his handsome face. "Keep it up, Dirk, and you'll kiss your way out of a job." She did her best to look stern, but the unrepentant grin he gave her made her turn away before she softened. "I'll expect a phone call from you as soon as you're finished interviewing Cora Johnson in North Dakota."

"Yes ma'am." He swatted her ass and left her office.

22

Teresa shared a knowing smirk with Hank when the chief ordered Dirk into her office. The guy had always been hard for directors to handle, and Teresa couldn't imagine how their boss was going to manage him at work and in a relationship.

Hank set his iPad on his desk. "Sterling isn't good at taking orders. Maybe he should go for a promotion; take a position as Chief Deputy somewhere."

Teresa snorted on her way to get them both a cup of coffee. "No way. He might not like taking orders, but he'd absolutely hate the paperwork and politics a chief has to deal with."

The chief's door opened, and Dirk emerged with his typical mischievous half-grin. The boss followed him out, but her face didn't hold the same humor. "Teresa, will you come in for a minute, please?"

She set her mug on her desk, and as she walked past Dirk, she murmured. "What did *I* do? You pissed her off and now we all have to pay the consequences."

Dirk chuckled. "Be brave."

Teresa entered the chief's office, and she gestured for her to close the door. Whatever this was about, it was the last thing Teresa needed right now. She was barely holding on as it was.

Chief Grey leaned back in her chair. "Have a seat."

It must be bad if she had to sit down for whatever was coming. Teresa perched on the edge of a chair in front of her boss's desk. "What's up?"

"That's exactly what I'm wondering. Are you feeling alright? Is everything okay at home?"

"I'm fine. Why do you ask?"

"You look tired."

Teresa's inner alarms went off. Where was this going? Did the chief think she was dropping the ball? "I didn't sleep very well last night. But don't worry. It won't affect my work."

Grey studied her for long seconds, and Teresa resisted fidgeting. "Your work is always exemplary. I never worry about that. It's just that... you can talk to me, you know. I'm not a mother, but I imagine being a single mom is incredibly hard, and I'm concerned you're taking care of everyone except for yourself."

Teresa's heart thudded heavily, and she rolled her lips between her teeth. "I'm fine. I've been dealing with some stuff with Tomas, but we'll get through it."

"You know our team is like a family and we're here for you, right?"

"Yeah, I guess. I mean, our private lives are still that, though."

"True, but what happens in our home lives impacts our work lives. With such a small team, it is inevitable."

"I'm sorry if you think I've been slacking."

Grey sprang forward and leaned on her desk. "I am not saying that at all. You never slack off. I'm saying I think you're struggling, and I want to help. I know we're not friends, but... we could be."

Teresa was too stunned to speak. "Uh... there's nothing..." She didn't have any real friends. There was no extra time for that. Dirk was the closest thing to a friend that she had. She knew he'd be there for her if she ever asked, but it wasn't like they were confidants.

"Listen," Grey went on. "Dirk and Henry are flying to Cheyenne today. I have a few meetings and some paperwork to do, but that's all. I can handle the phones. Why don't you take the rest of the day off? Do something nice for yourself—or at the very least, get a nap."

Her boss's smile held kindness and compassion and also what looked suspiciously like pity. Teresa's gut balled up with anxiety. "I don't want you to think I can't hack my job."

"I don't. Honestly. But we all need a break now and then and it never comes when we've scheduled vacation. I'm serious, Teresa. You need some rest, and today is the perfect time to take it."

"Okay. Thanks." Teresa stood. She wasn't sure she remembered how to relax, but she could use the time to stop in at Tomas's school for a surprise visit. She needed to have a conversation with his art teacher.

After the guys left for their trip, Teresa completed a combined data report on speculated travel dates and locations for Simeon Gryms over the past year, then left the office in time to have lunch with her son.

Teresa signed in as a visitor in the school office and went to the cafeteria to find Tomas. The room was loud, with children talking and laughing. Most kids brought their lunch from home, and Teresa wondered if the kids on the free lunch program, like Tomas, were the only ones who got the school lunch. The day's offering was fish sticks with ketchup, packaged applesauce, and milk. She shuddered, facing another place she was failing.

Tomas was not sitting at the table with his classmates, so she panned the room. Still, she didn't see him. So, she looked for him table by table. He was not in the cafeteria. She went back to the office to ask where her son was. Maybe he was in the principal's office.

On her way to the front of the school, she saw Tomas outside by the flagpole. He was talking with Ms. Frieza. Teresa moved behind a huge money tree plant and watched. The teacher looked happy, so it was unlikely that Tomas was in trouble. She handed him a folded paper, which he crammed in his back pocket, and then waved as he ran off to the playground. Strange.

Teresa hurried out a side door that opened to the playground. "Tomas!" she called and waved. "Tomas!"

Her son, hearing his name, looked around until he saw her. His face brightened, and he ran to her. "Hi, Mom. What are you doing here?"

"I came to have lunch with you, but you weren't in the cafeteria."

"You can play with me at recess. Want to swing?"

"I saw you out in front of the school with Ms. Frieza. What were you doing?"

"Oh, yeah. She asked me to do her a favor. Come on, Mom. Let's swing."

Teresa let her son pull her toward the swing set. "What kind of favor?"

"Just took a present to her friend."

Teresa pushed Tomas on the swings until the bell rang, and he had to line up for class. She went back to the office and asked if she could see the art teacher.

The office secretary called the art room, but no one answered, so she consulted a color-coded schedule. "Oh. That explains it, Ms. Frieza is off this afternoon. She'll be back on Friday. Can I leave her a message?"

"No, thanks." Teresa handed in her visitor's badge and left the school. She used her free afternoon to get some errands done, but her concern regarding her son's art teacher grew. Unable to shake the feeling that something was wrong, Teresa returned to the Marshals Office to research Ms. Holly Frieza.

It was after hours and the boss was gone, which was a relief. She had crafted an excuse to be in the office but was glad she didn't have to use it. On her work computer, she ran a background check on the teacher, but it revealed little. Frieza had had several traffic tickets along with one charge for minor drug possession of marijuana. Of course, she didn't like learning that, but it didn't raise any alarms. She shut down her computer and grabbed her purse.

As she reached for the office door, it swung inward and she gasped, "Chief!"

"Teresa!" Chief Grey pressed her hand against her chest. "You startled me. I thought I was the only one here."

"Sorry. I just stopped by to grab something I forgot. See you tomorrow."

Her boss's brows knitted as she stood to the side. Teresa brushed by her and hurried out the door. She took the stairs rather than wait for the elevator, not wanting to give Grey the chance to ask her any questions.

23

———————

H ank and Dirk sat in matching plaid and leather wing-back chairs facing Cora Johnson in her vaulted living room. Even though she obviously had money, Cora decorated her home with handmade cross stitch scenes and sayings. In her mid-forties, she still showed evidence of the attractive woman she had once been, but since then, her hair had grayed, and what were probably once voluptuous curves had expanded.

Cora poured them cups of tea they had already tried to decline without success. She passed a plate of snicker-doodles to Hank, which he accepted gratefully. He took two and handed them on to Dirk, who shook his head.

"Thank you, boys, for coming all the way up here from Billings. I can't tell you how shocked I was when I realized Don was actually a thieving murderer hunted by the authorities, you know?"

Shocked? Maybe. Thrilled? Definitely. Dirk accepted

the cup of tea Cora handed him. "What's the last name he's using? Do you have any recent photos of him?"

"Williams. Don Williams. Here's the photo I sent to your boss already but let me look for more on my phone." Cora scrolled through her images. "Oh, here's one. This is from the day we met. I took a picture of him when I added him to my contacts. I'd completely forgotten about it." She passed her phone to Dirk.

"Do you mind if I text this to my phone?"

"You betcha. I want to help you catch that scoundrel in any way I can."

Dirk performed the task and then gave her device to Hank. He studied the grinning face on the screen. The guy was Gryms, alright, though he looked very different with glasses and an old-fashioned haircut. Gryms could disguise himself, but he couldn't change his bone structure.

Hank texted the picture to his phone as well. "You don't even need facial recognition software to tell that this man is Simeon."

"I can't believe I didn't see it right away." Cora fluttered her fingers in the air as though batting away the unwanted truth. "I guess I didn't want to face it. But when my jewelry started showing up missing, I could no longer look the other way."

Hank gave her phone back. "Where did you say you met him?"

"At the library fundraiser dinner. He approached me after the auction."

"Did you bid on any auction items?"

Cora gave him a guilty smile. "Of course. It was a

fundraiser, dontcha know. I love libraries, and I'm always happy to support ours. I won an antique sterling silver tea set."

Dirk set his full cup and saucer on the coffee table. "Do you mind me asking how much the winning bid was?"

"Oh." She flapped her hand again. "I bid five-thousand dollars. I know the set wasn't worth that much, but I wasn't about to let Fanny Lind get it. She'd lord it over me for the rest of my days, dontcha know."

Hank shared a meaningful glance with his partner before he handed Cora back her phone. "Don approached you after you won the tea set?"

"Yes, he congratulated me."

"Did he say why he was in Bismarck?"

Dirk followed up. "And at a local library auction?"

Cora pursed her lips. "He said he was in town on business and didn't want to sit alone in his hotel room. He saw the event posted on the town hall marquis and decided to come on over." She gestured at Dirk's cup. "You better drink that up while it's still hot, hon."

Dirk rotated the cup a half turn. "Was yours the highest bid of the night?"

She breathed in and straightened her shoulders. "Why, yes, it was. Fanny tried to beat me out this year, but she just couldn't hold out."

Hank rolled his lips between his teeth to keep from smiling. He took a sip from the delicate China cup. "Do have any idea where Don is right now?"

"He told me he was going to look for a job today. That he didn't want me to have to support him." Cora's laugh was self-deprecating. "And then he asked me for fifty dollars. Oof, I can't believe I fell for him."

Dirk lifted a cookie from the plate. "Did he happen to say where he was looking? What type of work he does?"

"No, but he always ends his day at the Hoot'n and Holler bar at the edge of town. I'd be happy to give you directions."

"Thanks, but Hank can look it up on the navigation system in the car. We'll try to find him, but it's important that if he comes home before we do, you say nothing to him about his real identity or about us being here. And text me right away. So far, Gryms hasn't harmed any of the women he's taken advantage of, at least not physically. But the last time he felt trapped, he killed a man. We don't want him getting suspicious."

"Okey-dokey, then. I'll text you a note, for sure."

Hank looked up the address for the bar, and he and Dirk thanked Cora, assuring her they would be back to see her before they returned to Billings.

Half an hour later, Hank sat across from Dirk at a high-top table in the bar Cora sent them to. Hank took a long swallow of beer and was feeling his oats. He'd taken three trips in the last week that he didn't have to apologize to Amy for. In fact, he never even told her he left town. She didn't seem to care, anyway, and he'd felt incredibly free.

When the server came to check on them, Dirk ordered another IPA and Hank was about to follow suit when he decided to live on the edge. "How about a shot of Jack?"

Dark eyes studied him before Dirk raised a single sardonic brow. "Technically, we're working."

"*Technically*, it's five 'till five. By the time our drinks get here we'll be off. Come on, just one." When Dirk didn't object, Hank ordered a second beer and two shots of whiskey. When their drinks arrived, Hank held up the most recent photo of Gryms for the waitress to look at. "Have you ever seen this guy in here?"

She took his phone and held it close to her face. "Yeah, I've seen him. He comes in a couple of times a week. Why do you want to know?"

"Just looking for a friend."

The server shrugged and moved on to the next table. Hank tapped his shot on the table and waited for Dirk. They tossed back the liquid fire and soothed their scorched throats with swallows of ice-cold beer. "Here's to freedom."

Dirk's response was to study him with his inscrutable eyes. Hank hoped that one day he could hide his thoughts as well as his partner could. Amy always told him she could practically see everything he was thinking written on his face. Well, screw that. He downed his second beer.

He and Dirk scrutinized every face that came through the door. Two hours later, when Gryms still hadn't shown, they agreed to play pool with a couple of guys while they waited. Hank opened a tab and told the bartender to keep the drinks coming. Dirk was on his third beer when Hank lost count of his own. It felt good to relax and have fun knowing he had no one to answer to. And since it looked like Gryms was a no-show, Hank let his hair down.

He had lined up his pool cue for the next shot when a slender arm slid around his waist and squeezed. Hank tilted his head to see who the appendage belonged to and met the sapphire eyes of a woman with long brown curls. He chuckled. "Hello. Are you here to be my lucky charm? Or are you casting spells against me for the other team?"

The woman giggled. "Depends on how well you do on this shot. I only root for winners."

Hank had already lined up the shot, so without taking his eyes from hers, he struck the ball. "Green six, corner pocket." He grinned at the sound of the pool ball falling into the leather net.

The brunette clapped and bounced on her toes. "Nice shot! Looks like I am a lucky charm. Buy me a drink?"

Hank waved the server over. His charm asked for a dirty vodka martini, and he changed from drinking beer to double Old Fashioneds.

Dirk moved around to his side of the table and rubbed the end of his cue with a square of chalk. "You're hitting it pretty hard, kid. You might want to slow down."

"I'm just blowing off some steam. I'm fine."

"Who's your friend?" Dirk studied the woman hanging on him.

Hank laughed. "I don't know. What's your name, sweetheart?"

"I'm Linda." She held a delicate hand out to Dirk. "Linda, the lucky charm. Now tell me who you boys are."

"I'm Hank, and this is my partner, Dirk."

"Partner?"

"Well... friend. We're friends—right Dirk?" Hank nudged Dirk in the ribs with his elbow. "I think it's your turn, *friend*."

Dirk ran his fingers along his jaw before studying the pool table. "We should probably head to the hotel after this game." He aimed the cue ball at the red three.

"You go ahead. I'm gonna stay for a while. It's been too long since I've had so much fun."

Two rounds of drinks later, Linda and Hank had their arms draped around each other, and were laughing and flirting shamelessly. God only knew the last time he'd had such fun with a woman in a bar.

Dirk approached him with a pint glass filled with water. "Drink this, and then let's go."

Hank took the glass, peering at its contents with suspicion. "All right, *mother*." He laughed and downed the clear drink. "But I don't wanna go."

Dirk grasped him by the shoulders and leaned close to speak into his ear. "Look kid, I know it feels good to cut loose. But last I checked, you were still married to a woman you love. Say goodbye, and let's get out of here."

Hank's head swam, and he didn't want to think about Amy right then. Linda laughed at his jokes and complimented his pool play, his looks, and his muscles. And it felt damn good, especially when she ran her hands all over him. But Dirk closed the tab and dragged Hank out the door while he shouted goodbyes to his beautiful lucky charm.

The next thing Hank was aware of was waking up in a pitch-black room with someone knocking on the door. He grabbed a pillow and held it over his head to drown out the noise, but a voice called out in a loud whisper, "Hank, are you in there? It's Linda. This is your room, right?" She knocked again. "Hank, wake up. Let me in."

Hank rubbed his eyes with the heels of his hands and tried to think of who Linda was as he stumbled toward the voice. He flung open the door to the cute, dark-haired woman he'd met at the bar. "Linda?" He blinked to clear his fuddled brain, but it didn't help.

The brunette pushed her way past him into the room as his mind strained to make sense of what was happening. His tongue stuck to the roof of his Sahara-dry mouth, and thirst won out for his attention over his curiosity. He filled a cup with water and guzzled it down in one gulp.

"Here, I brought this for us." Linda held up a fifth of Jack Daniels. She cracked open the seal and poured his glass to the brim.

Blinking the sleep from his eyes, Hank cocked his head and asked, "What are you doing here? How did you find me?"

"I followed you, silly. I knew you didn't want the night to end, but your Big Brother had other plans. So, now he's in bed and here we are." She poured a little Jack into another glass and clinked it against his. "Want to play strip poker?"

Hank couldn't get his mind to focus on what was happening. He looked down and noticed all he had on was a pair of shorts. "I think I'd lose that game pretty quick." He set his glass down on the dresser. "Listen, Linda..."

She picked up the brimming glass and handed it to him. "OK, so... no strip poker. How about we drink to new friendships." She tapped her glass against his again, and they both drank. "And a toast to the best pool player I've ever seen?"

Hank chuffed. "Hardly." But he drank with her, anyway.

Linda turned the TV on to a music channel and danced in sultry movements around the room. Hank drained his glass as he watched her. He shook his head against the forbidden thoughts forming in his imagination, but the abrupt move made him queasy, and he sat down on the edge of the bed. He'd had way too much to drink and just wanted to crash. But Linda danced toward him. She swung a leg over his and sat straddling his lap.

She looped her arms around his neck and kissed him. He knew it was wrong to let her do it, but he didn't stop her. Maybe it didn't count if he didn't kiss her back, he rationalized. His internal argument soon became a moot point.

Linda spoke against his lips. "I heard you guys asking about some man when we were at the bar. A guy named Simeon Gryms?"

"Yeah?" He needed to put a stop to this before it went too far. Grabbing her arms, he untangled them from his neck. She pushed him backward onto the bed and followed him down, landing on his chest.

"Tell me what you know about Gryms and why you're looking for him." She slid her hand down between them, spiking the neurotransmitters in his brain to full dopamine overload. His heart pounded, but cotton filled his head and clouded out all rational thought.

24

———

Laurie hadn't heard from Dave ever since Dirk chased him off the other night. She'd been disappointed when he didn't stay for a nightcap, but she understood since Dirk had made it clear he wasn't leaving. Worried that Dave might have given up on her, she decided to invite him over for dessert and coffee. Caleb went to bed at 8:00 pm and after that, they could have the rest of the evening together, alone.

Laurie texted Dave. **U busy tonight?**

Dave: **Not if you have something planned :)**

Laurie: **How does dessert and coffee sound at my place? 7:30?**

Dave: **Sounds great, can't wait. See u then.**

Well, that was easy. Now to decide what to bake and what to wear. Laurie liked Dave a lot and hoped he felt the same. She was relieved Dirk was out of town. There was no chance he could interrupt them from North Dakota with his mis-placed big brother act.

She and Caleb had tacos for dinner, and Laurie made

sure she had everything cleaned up including her son by seven. Caleb looked so sweet and cozy in his flannel Scooby-Doo pajamas, curled up next to Bear playing with his Legos. Laurie took a cherry pie out of the oven and set it on a cooling rack and joined Caleb on the floor in front of the fireplace. Winter was in the air and the cheery flame warmed the room.

Her nerves skittered when the doorbell rang. "That must be Mr. Dave." She pushed herself up from the floor.

"Why is he here at bedtime?" Caleb's big blue eyes gazed up in question.

"Mommy and Mr. Dave are going to visit after you go to bed, sweetheart." She crossed the room and opened the door. "Hi. Come on in, it's freezing out there. The temperature really took a drop today, didn't it?"

Dave stepped in, bending to kiss her on the cheek. "Winter's at the door." He looked into the living room. "That's a nice fire. Hi Caleb." He took off his coat and hung it on the coat tree by the front door.

"Go warm up by the fireplace, and I'll start the coffee." Laurie went to the kitchen.

Dave rubbed his hands together near the fire before kneeling on the carpet next to Caleb. A low warning rumble echoed from Bear's throat. The muscle-bound rottweiler got up and squeezed himself between the man and the boy. Dave took the hint and scooted over to give the dog room.

"I don't think your dog likes me very much," he called to Laurie.

She returned to the living room with two steaming mugs and sat on the couch. "Why do you say that?"

"He growls at me every time I'm here."

"He's just protective of us. He'll get used to you the more you're around."

Dave grinned. "Is that an open invitation?"

Laurie's pulse leapt. "You're always welcome."

"I've noticed Bear doesn't have any problem with Sterling."

"That's because he's known Dirk since he was a puppy. In fact, it was Dirk and his good friend Caitlin Reed, a deputy marshal K9 handler from Wyoming, who brought Bear for Caleb to help him cope after Sam died. Bear doesn't know you yet, that's all."

"If you say so." Dave moved to sit next to her on the sofa.

"Hey little man," Laurie addressed her son. "It's time to get ready for bed. Go potty and brush your teeth and I'll be in to read your story in just a minute."

"But I want pie, too," he whined.

"Not this close to bedtime. You can have a piece after lunch tomorrow. Deal?"

"I guess." Caleb got up and tromped down the hall toward the bathroom with Bear on his heels.

Laurie refilled Dave's coffee. "Make yourself at home, I won't be long." She went to read Caleb a book and tuck him in for the night. Bear took his place on the quilt at the foot of Caleb's bed.

"Sorry about that." Returning to the living room, Laurie swept her fingers across Dave's shoulders as she rounded the couch. "But I thought it would be better if Caleb didn't need a babysitter. This way there's no chance of being interrupted by anyone."

"Unless Dirk drives by and sees my car."

Laurie's cheeks warmed. "Don't worry, he's in North Dakota." She laughed softly. "I'll just get us that pie."

They shared stories of their day over pie and ice cream. And when they were finished, Dave rested his arm around her shoulders while they sipped their coffee. Laurie snuggled close. This was exactly how she imagined their perfect evening.

"Speaking of Sterling, what's he doing in North Dakota?"

"I think they're still tracking that Gryms guy."

"Ah, that's right. How's his other case going? The Crandall case?"

Laurie released a sigh. The last thing she wanted to do was get into a conversation about Dirk. "You just saw him the other night. I'm sure nothing much has changed."

"You're probably right. I just know how frustrated he was when Crandall escaped. And Sterling's the kind of guy who doesn't let things like that go."

Remorse over her selfish attitude made her answer his question more fully. "He mentioned something about talking to Marco, a friend of his and Sam's in Interpol. Something Africa. I'm not sure. You should call Dirk if you want to know more. Honestly, he doesn't talk a lot about work, and I didn't really listen to the details."

"Africa?" Dave frowned.

"I think that's what he said, but I could be wrong. It might have been Asia. He just mentioned it in passing, and then we talked about Caleb's new school." Laurie set her coffee cup on the table and leaned against Dave's chest.

He kissed her forehead and lifted her chin to kiss her mouth. Hunger for him flared in her belly. The intensity of their desire grew, and Dave eased her backward onto the couch. She slid her arms around his neck.

Dave glanced down the hall. "Is this okay? I mean with Caleb in the other room?"

Laurie's words floated out on her breath. "He sleeps like the dead, but... let's go to my room. We can lock the door."

The amber flecks in Dave's eyes deepened, and he kissed her once more before he lifted her from the sofa. "Which way?"

At one o'clock in the morning, Dave slid his arm out from under her head, waking her. Missing his heat, she reached for him. He wove his fingers together with hers and kissed her before pulling the covers up to her chin.

"I better go. I don't want to be here in the morning when Caleb wakes up."

Laurie sighed. He was right, of course, but she wished he could stay. "He won't be awake for at least five more hours."

"Tempting. But, if I don't go now, I'll be too tired to drive." Dave pulled on his jeans and buttoned his shirt before sitting on her side of the bed. He gave her a lingering kiss. "Tonight was amazing, Laurie."

When he bent to put on his shoes, she slid out of bed and wrapped herself in her robe. They walked hand in hand down the hallway toward the living room. Dave gathered their dirty pie plates and carried them to the kitchen.

"Thanks for the dessert." He grinned. "You were delicious."

"You're welcome. You could always stay for another… slice." Laurie giggled and slid her arms around his waist."

He kissed her, and chuckling, he pulled away. "You have no idea how much I want to, but I forgot to send a report to my SAC. I was supposed to do it this afternoon. He wanted it by five."

"Can't you send it from your phone?"

"No. It's classified information that I can't have on my personal devices." He squeezed her tight, kissing her cheek, then her ear, and whispered, "I really want to stay."

"I understand. Work comes first." Disappointment wrapped around her like a cloak. "Can I see you tomorrow?" Laurie ran her fingers along his stubbly jaw.

"Try and stop me."

25

It was dark when Teresa left the office. When she picked Tomas up at the school, she unzipped his backpack to put in his water bottle. Inside the flap, an envelope with Tomas's name on it piqued her interest. Her son was putting blocks away, so she opened the card which said, "Thanks kiddo!" and inside was a five-dollar bill.

When they got home, she turned to Tomas. "Did you say Ms. Frieza asked you to take a note to a friend of hers today?"

"Yeah." Tomas fidgeted in his seat.

"Did she pay you to do that?"

"Not really." He couldn't meet her eye. "I told her you said she couldn't give me anymore more toys, so she wanted to give me money."

"We don't take money for doing favors, Tomas."

"I know, but I'm saving for Mario Kart!" His earnest face broke her heart.

"You have nothing to play Mario Kart on. Besides, that doesn't change anything. Where was this friend of Ms. Frieza's?"

"At Seven-Eleven."

The words hit Teresa like a physical blow. "What? Seven-Eleven? You left school grounds? By yourself?" She paced, needing movement to manage her anger.

"It's not very far. It's just around the corner."

Teresa stood, shaking her head and breathing to steady herself. "You are *never* to leave school without my permission. Ms. Frieza was wrong to ask you to do that."

Tomas crumpled in his chair. She knew he believed he was doing his teacher a favor and was excited that he made some money at the same time. To him, it was no big deal, but Teresa was ready to explode. She sucked in another deep breath.

"I'm going to call Mrs. Fox from next door and see if she can watch you for a little while. I need to run an errand." While she waited for her neighbor to come, Teresa did a Google search for Holly Frieza's address. It was time to confront the woman who was messing with her son.

Teresa left Tomas doing his homework with Mrs. Fox and drove across town to Ms. Frieza's home. She located the address and parked across the street, one house down. Sitting in her car, she took a few minutes to gather her thoughts about what she wanted to say. When she was ready, Teresa reached for the latch. But the front door of the teacher's house opened, and the woman in question came out. She got into the car in the drive and backed out, speeding off in the other direction. Teresa followed.

Ms. Freiza drove directly to the neighborhood housing Tomas's elementary school, but instead of pulling in there, she went to the Seven-Eleven around the corner. Teresa rolled into the parking lot after her but remained in the shadows at the back and watched Ms. Frieza through the glass storefront.

The young woman entered the store and went directly to the refrigerators along the wall to get a soda. She wandered the aisles until the one other customer left. Then she beelined to the register where it looked like she and the clerk argued. The man reached under the counter and retrieved a brick-sized package wrapped in brown paper. Holly Frieza gestured at him, and he took out a pocketknife and punctured the wrapping. He dipped the blade inside and held it to his nose and sniffed.

Frieza seemed to relax, and she thrust cash at the man before clutching the parcel to her chest. Teresa recognized a drug deal when she saw one and opened the gun safe in her car's console. She grabbed her pistol, and jumping out of her car, she sprinted through the double glass doors. "Don't move!" she shouted as she ran inside. "Everybody keep your hands where I can see them."

Two sets of eyes stared at her. Holly Frieza stood motionless with her mouth open, but the clerk recovered from the shock and reached under the counter. He pulled out a shotgun and aimed it at the teacher. "Just back on out of here, lady. Or I'll kill her. You don't want to make me do that, now do you?"

Teresa leveled her gun at the man. "I'm Deputy US Marshal Mendez. I suggest you lower your weapon. At this point, all we have here is a minor drug deal. Let's not add murder to the mix. Drop the gun."

Holly's eyes shifted and widened, so it shouldn't have surprised Teresa when the hard muzzle of a handgun tapped the back of her head.

"No, Deputy. You drop *your* gun." A male voice with a smoker's rasp scraped against her neck.

Teresa's heart sank to her boots as adrenaline spikes nipped along her nerves. She had screwed up and got herself into this mess by rushing in on emotion. She knew better, but had allowed her anger to take the lead, anyway. Now she saw no way out. She could try to disarm the main behind her, but Holly would get shot for sure.

The drug dealers couldn't afford to let either of them live. There wasn't much she could do but watch for an opportunity of present itself. She had run off half-cocked wanting to protect Tomas, and now she couldn't see a way out of this. Tomas would be alone in the world without a mother. With no one.

Tears flowed down Holly's face while Teresa ground her teeth to control her fear. "Listen. How about we all calm down and lower our guns at the same time? You can take the money and leave. My keys are in my car. I can't follow you. That way, you get what you want without adding the murder of an innocent woman and a federal marshal to the charges."

"Nice try, Deputy. But both of you can describe us, and that won't do." The man who held her spoke with an eerie calmness. "Jimmy, take her gun."

The clerk lowered the shotgun and came around the counter. He grabbed Teresa's gun from her hand. The man behind her shoved her forward into Holly, who dropped the drugs on the floor.

"Good. Now, Jimmy, grab the smack. This is a win-win for us." As Jimmy did as he was told, the leader pushed the women toward the back room.

Without warning, the back door slammed open, and two armored SWAT officers burst through. One grabbed hold of Holly and, throwing her down, covered her with his body. Teresa dove to the side as the man behind her fired his weapon. He received two shots to the chest and one to the head in return. Jimmy dropped the cash and the brick of coke and threw his hands in the air.

Teresa rolled to her feet and came face to face with Emory Grey, striding into the shop behind the SWAT team wearing a helmet and tactical vest.

"Chief?" Teresa couldn't make sense of what she saw.

Her boss returned her weapon to her. "Hang on to this the next time, Mendez."

Stunned beyond comprehension, Teresa uttered, "Yes, ma'am."

The women didn't speak until the local cops took control of the crime scene and the suspects and allowed Teresa to leave. She clutched Chief Grey's arm as they walked toward their cars. "How did you know I was here? That I needed help?"

Grey stopped in the middle of the lot and faced her. "I figured you could use a friend, so on my way home from work, I picked up some ice cream and thought I would stop by and maybe we could have a bowl together. But when I turned onto your street, I saw you run out the door and speed away in your car. Instinct told me something was wrong and that I should follow you. Seems like it was a good thing I did."

"I don't know what to say."

"Say you'll never go into a situation like that without backup, ever again. I know you're a little rusty, but that was a rookie move."

Teresa fought the tears with all her stubborn might, but they dripped from her eyes. The stress she'd been under finally winning the battle as a sob broke from her throat.

Grey flung an arm around her shoulders and marched them toward her car. "Come on. Let's get out of here before you fall apart."

Teresa was grateful. She couldn't stomach the idea of dissolving into tears before the SWAT officers. Grey asked a uniform to drive Teresa's car to her house, and she took Teresa home.

The ice cream was a melted mess, so they had wine instead. "I'm such an idiot. I've been screwing up everything lately." Teresa explained all that had happened to put her in the deadly situation she'd found herself in that night.

"I knew you were stressed, but I didn't know how bad it was."

"Thanks for looking out for me, Chief. Tomas could have wound up without a mom, which is way worse than a stressed one."

"I've always got your back. Just like you would have mine. And call me Emory. We've gone through enough together now to be on a first name basis. I hope you consider me a friend."

"Thanks. I don't have many of those. Just you and the guys."

"Yeah. We make a pretty good family, I think."

26

Hank drifted through oblivion until more banging crashed inside his brain. This time, his head pounded with each sharp rap. He held his throbbing skull between his hands. "Coming!" he growled.

"I brought coffee." Dirk's voice sounded through the crack.

"Thank God." Hank opened the door.

Dirk reached in and flipped on the light. "It smells like a distillery in here. Did you empty the room bar?" Dirk held out a steaming cup but fell short of giving it to him. "You've got to be kidding me."

Hank followed Dirk's gaze to the bed where a dark-haired woman sat brushing hair out of her eyes. The shock woke him fully. "I—"

"It's Linda, right?" Dirk picked her shirt up off the floor and tossed it to her.

Hank's stomach threatened to pitch its contents. This

could not be right. He wasn't that guy. Was he? He stumbled into the bathroom and splashed cold water on his face. Behind him, he heard Linda talking to Dirk.

"You don't have to worry about your friend. He passed out." She reached for the door. "Some guys just can't hold their liquor. See you, Hank." And with that, she was gone.

DIRK KEPT his mouth shut about Hank's personal affairs. He wasn't the kid's priest. It wasn't up to him to judge what Hank did or didn't do. Even if he had an opinion. They spent the day following leads, no matter how small, trying to find Gryms's trail.

Hank was hungover and rested his head against the cool car window as they drove. "I feel like such a dick. I'm sorry about last night."

Dirk side-eyed him. "You don't have to apologize to me. You're a grownup. What you do is your own business."

"Yeah, but you probably think I'm a total asshole."

"If I thought that, I'd have already said so."

"I've never... I didn't...God—I can't even say that for sure. I don't remember much after that chick showed up in my room."

"She said nothing happened."

"Yeah. Still, I let her think something would, or she wouldn't have come."

Dirk let the silence speak his agreement with Hank's assessment. A lecture on past behavior would not help him.

"It's just that I was having so much fun. I haven't relaxed and had a good time in so long, I can't remember. I felt so free, not having to check in and grovel about the fact that I had to travel for my job." Hank scrubbed his face with his hands. "If nothing happened, do you think I have to tell Amy about this? I was drunk. None of it meant anything."

Dirk pulled in a deep breath. He'd been on the receiving end of an unfaithful spouse, and he had strong feelings about it. Hannah had claimed she was drunk, too. That excuse meant nothing. But this wasn't about him and Hannah. This was Hank—his partner and friend. *He* was the one Dirk was loyal to. "Depends on what you consider as 'nothing happened'."

"You don't believe it?"

"It doesn't matter what I believe. The two of you spent the evening tongue-wrestling at the bar, and she spent the night in your room. You were both practically naked when I got there this morning. So, whether or not you had sex, I wouldn't say 'nothing happened.' Would you?"

"You think I should tell Amy, don't you?" Hank's statement sounded defeated.

"Would you want to know if she was the one in this situation?"

"She's pregnant."

"So? My question stands."

"I don't know. Maybe not. I mean, if nothing happened, then telling each other about it would just cause more trouble. More pain."

Dirk really didn't want to get into all this with Hank, but damn if he didn't care about the kid. "I think the bigger question is why any of it happened in the first place."

Hank flopped his head back against the seat. "I know." He sat quietly for several miles before he continued. "Things between Amy and me are broken. I don't know if we can fix them or not. It doesn't seem like she wants to, and honestly, I'm not sure I do either—anymore. But..."

Waiting for Hank to finish his thought, Dirk turned toward the airport. It was almost time for their flight home. Finally, when Hank didn't continue, he prodded. "But... what?"

"But... There's a baby to think about now."

It was 7:00 pm by the time Dirk and Hank landed in Billings. Together, they drove to Dirk's house. Hank was still feeling rough and wanted nothing but to go straight to bed. Dirk left him to his own devices and called Emory.

"Hey, we just got home. Can I see you tonight? Or is it too late?"

"I was hoping you would call. I'm on my way home now. Do you want me to come there?"

Dirk chuffed at the irony of having to explain himself. "Hank's staying at my house. So, it would probably be better for me to come there."

"Works for me. I'll put on something comfortable." Her seductive tone swirled around his heart like smoke.

"I'll be right there."

"Wait." She laughed. "You didn't tell me how your trip went."

"We can talk about it later. Much later." He ended the call.

Dirk glanced at the clock on Emory's nightstand. It was one in the morning, and Em was curled up next to him, her head resting on his chest.

"Now that it's much later, will you tell me how it went in North Dakota?" Her breath tickled when she spoke. "And then I'll tell you about the excitement Teresa and I had."

"We are definitely on Gryms's trail, and we're getting close. I asked the local sheriff to drive by Cora Johnson's house through the night to keep an eye on her. She doesn't believe he'll return, but you never know."

"What do you think?"

"She's probably right. His pattern is to take off as soon as anyone gets suspicious, and she confronted him about her missing jewelry. That was only two days ago. We're closer now than we ever have been."

Emory rolled on top of him and propped her chin on her palm. "Not that I'm not thrilled that you did... but why did you come home if you're so close?"

"We couldn't pick up his trail, and besides, Hank needs to be home in Billings now. If the sheriff turns up anything, I'll go back right away. Otherwise, it's a waiting game."

"Things aren't any better between Henry and Amy?"

"No." Dirk reached for his glass of wine and finished it. Emory studied his face, but thankfully chose not to ask any more questions. "You said you and Teresa had some excitement. What happened?"

Emory told him how she'd suspected Teresa was under too much stress and had wanted to reach out to her in friendship. And how her gesture turned into a drug bust.

"I can't believe Teresa put herself in such a dangerous position." He'd worked with T in the field. She had never been so careless.

"She's tapped out. Teresa's working hard to wear all the hats, and when things went south with Tomas at school, she lost it. She needs our support right now. I'm going to squeeze the budget and see if I can get her a cost-of-living raise. It's got to be so hard to be a single parent."

"I could be better about checking in with her. Maybe I can take Tomas and Caleb out to learn duck hunting or something."

"She could use the break." She stretched to kiss the tip of his nose. "I'm glad you came home tonight. I've missed you."

"Me too. Seems like we've been bumping heads a lot lately." He kissed her and rolled her onto her back.

A soft giggle brought a smile to her lips. "Let's continue this in the morning. We'd better get some sleep if we're going to be any good at work tomorrow."

"We could always call in sick."

"Both of us on the same day? No way." She pushed him over to his side of the bed and snuggled up against him. "Besides, we've got work to do. You have a trap to set and that will need all your focus."

Her acknowledgement of his hunt for Crandall made him smile, and powerful emotions flooded through him.

She was the perfect woman for him, even when she was infuriating. "Emory?"

"Hmm?" She was already drifting.

"I love you."

27

———

Beaux sat on the deck of his Ferretti yacht amid a raucous party. This week he hosted a group of Chinese business executives who, once they arrived on his island, forgot entirely about the business at hand. A titillating orgy spontaneously conjugated in the main cabin, but Beaux was not in the mood. Melancholy rested on his shoulders like an old crone's shawl, so he went outside to watch the sunset. A perfect orange-gold ball dropped from the cerulean sky and seemed to bounce on the horizon before, like a breath, disappearing. Leaving faint streaks of glitter, the only evidence of its spectacular presence.

Sighing, Beaux hoisted his girth out of the lounge chair on the deck and made his way to the gangplank to disembark. He padded up the beach to his elaborate home. After rinsing the sand from his feet, he mounted the sweeping stairway that led to his bedroom. Sitting on the mattress next to his nightstand he opened the top drawer and retrieved an envelope filled with photos. The first one on the stack always made him smile. It depicted Troy and him when they were about 13 or 14 holding a fish they had caught in the Cane River. It was perhaps the only pure moment of boyhood innocence they shared. His favorite snapshot in time.

It surprised Beaux how much he missed Troy. He had never thought of himself as a man of deep feelings. He had no other friendships—no other relationships of any kind other than business. There was no one he truly trusted. Beaux sifted through the photos, selecting a few he would copy and send to Troy's mother and a few he wanted framed.

Chinara, Beaux's Nigerian slave, entered his suite and silently walked across the marble floor. She kneeled at his feet and bowed her head, awaiting his command. He didn't feel up to using the girl, but perhaps he'd make her give him a massage. Anything to rid himself of the blue emotions threatening to drown him.

"Chinara, take these photos down to Adebayo. Tell him to copy them and return them to me. Then I want a rub down before I go to bed."

She took the pictures and left the room without ever meeting his eye. He expected her coldness, but Beaux couldn't help wondering what it would be like to have a woman who wanted him, who was happy to see him. What would it feel like to be truly loved? He caught sight of his image in the mirror and scoffed at himself.

"You're getting soft, old man," he grumbled at his reflection.

He lay on the bed waiting for Chinara to return and remembered there was one woman who cared for him.

One who looked at him with admiration. Troy's mother —Maria Cortez—was the only connection he had left to his dear friend. Beaux was determined to take care of her until the end of her days.

He suddenly wanted very much to hear her voice. Beaux lifted the receiver of the elegant gold and ivory phone standing on his night table and dialed the number in Mexico.

The phone rang three times before Maria answered. "Hola?"

"Hola, Maria. It's Beaux Crandall. How are you doing?"

"Oh, Mr. Beaux. I'm so thankful you have called."

"I've been thinking of Troy and wanted to hear your voice. I found some more pictures of your son that I think you'll like." He told her about the day he and Troy had gone fishing and the fond memories he had of her son.

"I treasure seeing that photo as with all your others." The line went silent long enough that Beaux wondered if he had dropped the call. Finally, she spoke again. "I have had some bad news. I wasn't feeling well, and so I used some of the money you sent me to go to the doctor."

"Is everything alright? Do you need more money? I will wire some right away."

"Perhaps, but I'm not sure exactly what I will need in the coming days. The doctor says I have cancer."

"We'll get you a second opinion. The doctors could be wrong." Panic stirred in Beaux's belly. If he lost Maria, he'd be truly alone.

"It could be, but I doubt it. I am very sick, Mr. Beaux."

Beaux rose to his feet as sweat gathered on his forehead. "What can I do? Tell me everything you need."

"I don't think there's anything you can do. There's nothing anyone can do. But I would love to meet you in person before I die. Then I will know I'm not leaving this world alone."

Beaux wiped his face with his sleeve. "Yes, I will come. I am hosting business guests until Friday, but then I will be there." He suddenly cared very much about another person and wanted to see her, to honor her wishes and to honor his friend, her son. "I'll be there on Saturday afternoon. What can I bring you?"

"Just your friendship and your memories of my son."

When Chinara returned, she caught him wiping the tears from his eyes. She did not ask what was wrong. She had no compassion for him. For some reason, that surprised him. He accepted the photographs from her along with his Dawa night cap that he liked so much. But then he dismissed her. She only reminded him of his loneliness.

As he got into bed, his cell phone rang. Very few people had the number, so he reached for it. "This better be good news."

"It's important news. There's an active investigation into this phone line. The heat is on, and world-wide authorities are searching for you in Africa."

"I'll over-night my device to a man I know who lives near the Black Sea and tell him toss the device in the water. That ought to confuse the hell out of them. Especially if they are looking for me in Africa." Beaux chuckled. His subterfuge worked.

"They traced your phone to Morocco. I suppose they have to start somewhere."

"They can search all they want, but they'll never find me. Besides, I'm going on a little vacation, and I won't be anywhere near their hunt."

"Good. But I thought you'd want to know what's going on with the federal agencies. They haven't forgotten about you."

"No, I don't suppose they will. It would help if you dug up some dirt on the agents still hunting for me. Then they, like you, could be made to see that it's much better to have me as a friend than an enemy."

"I made one mistake, and you make me pay for it over and over again."

"I don't think it was a mistake. You are simply enjoying yourself. You can't help it if your superiors wouldn't see it the same way." Beaux laughed. "Don't be discouraged. When you have some time off, come to the island. Live out your fantasies. You may as well, since your appetite keeps you indebted to me whether you enjoy it or not. I'll send you my new phone number when I get one. Until then, keep your eyes and ears open." Beaux ended the call.

He finished his drink and pulled back the covers on his bed, laughing at the fact that he would be on the other side of the globe when the FBI and similar authorities were in Africa, hoping to catch him. He wished he could somehow watch them chase their tails in the wind.

28

———

Emory woke early to leave for the office. If there was one thing that wasn't perfect about the woman, it was that she was a morning person —a cheery, talkative, energetic, conquer-the-world type. Dirk glanced at the clock. "Four-thirty? You've got to be kidding me." He rolled over, tugging a pillow with him, covering his head to drown out the light and sounds she made getting ready for the day.

"Sorry to wake you. I like to get my workout in early, or I won't do it." She lifted a corner of the pillow and kissed his cheek. "I'll see you at work."

He groaned in response and drifted back to sleep.

The alarm on his watch went off at seven. Even then, he wished he could snooze another hour, but he rolled out of bed and turned on the shower. That and a couple of strong cups of coffee would set him right for the day.

He arrived at the office a little before eight, but behind Teresa. "Morning, T."

"Hey, Dirk." She smirked at him. "You look like you

could use a few more hours of sleep. How's the new puppy?"

Dirk chuffed at her reference to Hank. "He's settling in." He didn't feel the need to explain that it hadn't been his house guest that kept him up the night before. The culprit's office door was closed. "The boss in?"

"Yeah. She got a call a few minutes ago and shut her door to take it."

"I heard about all the excitement you two had last night."

Teresa dropped her chin and tinkered with some paperclips on her desk. "Yeah. I screwed up. I know."

"Listen up, T. Everybody makes mistakes. Hopefully, you'll learn from yours. It isn't just that you should have called for backup at the Seven-Eleven. It's that you should have asked for back up way before then, from us —your team. You don't have to struggle all on your own, you know."

Tears formed in Teresa's eyes, and she angrily swiped them away. "I'd be dead if the chief hadn't followed me. I can't believe I was such an idiot."

"Knock it off, Mendez. There's a lot of times I would have been dead if a fellow Marine or marshal didn't cover my ass. Beating yourself up about it won't do any good. Learn and move forward. But remember that you have family here that you work with every day, and speaking of that, I'd like to take Tomas and Caleb to a duck blind and teach them how to call in the birds sometime if that's okay with you."

Teresa's stormy expression brightened. "He'd love that. Tomas needs good men in his life."

"He's a great kid. I'll let you know when I can make it happen." Dirk stifled a yawn and, after tossing his leather jacket on his chair, went to pour a cup of coffee. He almost spilled it down his shirt when Emory's door burst open. "Dirk, I'm glad you're here. I just got word that Cora Johnson, the woman you and Henry interviewed in North Dakota, was murdered."

"What happened?" He set the brimming mug on his desk.

"The local cops are investigating. All they know at this point is a friend found her dead in her home. Someone crushed the back of her skull."

"Gryms. Probably in retaliation for talking to us. Damn it!" Dirk was suddenly sharply awake. He yanked out his phone and called Hank. "Where are you? We have to leave for Bismarck as soon as you get here, so hurry."

Emory stepped toward him, her hand reaching out before she thought better of it and dropped it to her side. "I'm sorry. I know you wanted to work on your operation in Mexico today."

"I'll organize it while we're in transit. Teresa?"

"Already on it. A USMS helicopter will pick you guys up at the airport in thirty minutes. I'll call Hank and reroute him to meet you there."

"Thanks, T." Dirk tilted his head toward Emory's office. She led the way inside, and following her, he closed the door behind him. He took her face in his hands and kissed her. "I'll see you soon."

"Be vigilant. This guy is unpredictable."

"Always." He turned to go.

"And Dirk—" He paused to glance over his shoulder. "I love you, too."

DURING THE AIRLIFT TO BISMARCK, Dirk organized "Operation Bait-and-Switch" to take place in Mexico on Saturday. He coordinated with ATF and ICE agents already operating in the area. An ATF agent and friend of his, John Garcia, who was stationed in Mexico City, agreed to inform and coordinate the mission locally with the Mexican National Guard and the Policía Federal. Dirk was waiting on Marco Agosti, his Interpol contact, to send him Crandall's final flight plan information, but he wanted all the players to be in place and ready to move when the moment came.

It seemed only minutes before they touched down in Bismarck. A black Explorer waited for them to the side of the landing pad, and Dirk and Hank drove to Cora Johnson's house. The crime scene was buzzing with cops, detectives, and emergency medical personnel. A crowd of looky-loos milled around outside the yellow crime-scene tape. Dirk honked to get the onlookers to move aside so he could park. They hopped out of the SUV and found the officer tasked with maintaining the security of the scene.

"US Marshals." Dirk showed the uniformed cop his badge. They signed into the scene, and after sliding paper booties over their shoes, they entered the house. Crime Scene Investigators were everywhere, taking pictures, measuring, and dusting for fingerprints.

Dirk approached the detective in-charge, and he and Hank presented their identification again. "We're tracking a guy named Simeon Gryms. You may remember the shooting of the armored car guard down in Denver?"

The detective nodded. "Yeah, I remember hearing about that on the news. You think he's our killer?"

"Could be. We were up here yesterday interviewing Ms. Johnson. Gryms tangled her up in his usual con. Gryms likes living large off the bank accounts of lonely, wealthy women. When Ms. Johnson noticed some of her jewelry missing, she confronted him, and he took off. And now, after talking to us, she is dead. Seems like too much to be a coincidence."

"Okay, yeah. Gotcha. How can we help?"

"Have you recovered the murder weapon?"

"Yup, we think so. Our officer found a large plumbing wrench on the floor next to the body. They'll be checking for prints, you know. Is the guy you're looking for in the national database?"

"Yes, so if you're lucky enough to find prints, we'll have confirmation." Dirk handed him his business card. "Let me know if you find any concrete evidence. We're going to talk to the neighbors. See if anyone heard or saw anything."

"Our uniforms are already out doing that."

"Good. We'll join the ranks, then. Keep me posted about what you learn. We need to catch this guy before he kills again."

"Gotcha. Will do."

Dirk and Hank left the house and stopped on the

front porch to assess the crowd of onlookers and the neighborhood street. A man wearing a dark gray coat over a black hoodie stood at the back of the gathering and caught Dirk's eye.

"See the hooded guy with the sunglasses at eleven o'clock?"

"Roger that. Looks shifty, for sure. Wonder what he's nervous about?"

"Let's have a chat with him and find out." Dirk turned to his left and Hank tracked to the right, circling around to approach him from opposite sides.

The hooded man watched the investigation proceedings with great interest, along with the others waiting for the ambulance to arrive and collect the body. Hank slowed as he approached the onlookers and blended in with the crowd at the fringe. Dirk was still fifty yards away from the other side of the gathering but kept himself from rushing. He pretended to be texting as though he wasn't paying attention to the people he approached and opened his camera app, flipping the lens toward himself. Once he reached the group, he moved to the front and held his phone up like he was videotaping the stretcher carrying the black body bag as it came out of the house. Instead, he snapped photo after photo of the suspicious-looking man behind him.

Hank shifted gradually closer, but something spooked their target. The hooded man eased away from the crowd, walking with false calmness down the street. Suddenly, he took off running, and Dirk sprinted after him. Hank pushed his way through the people and was on Dirk's heels in seconds.

Dirk shouted, "Stop! US Marshals!"

The man yanked a handgun from his coat and without looking, aimed behind him, shooting wildly before darting between two parked cars. Both deputies unholstered their weapons and sped after him as he ran down the sidewalk and through the front lawns of homes on the street.

Three houses up, a young woman wearing headphones came out of her house dressed for a run. Adrenaline fueled Dirk's endurance. They had to reach the guy before he got to her.

"Go back inside!" Dirk yelled, but the runner couldn't hear him over her music.

Ten years younger and twice as fast, Hank passed Dirk. He gained on the suspect and dove to tackle him.

Shots fired from behind them, and Dirk spun to see who was shooting. A woman with a brown ponytail pulled through the back of a baseball cap was on their flank. Was she an undercover cop? He couldn't tell, but he and Hank were potentially in her line of fire. When she leveled her weapon to shoot again, Dirk lunged at her, knocking her to the ground before she caught Hank with a stray bullet.

"What the hell?" Recognizing her, he tugged the gun from her hand. "What do you think you're doing?"

"That's him, isn't it? That's Simeon Gryms. He killed my brother, and he will not get away with it."

"Who is your brother?" Dirk rolled the woman to her belly, cuffed her wrists, and pulled her to her feet.

"Gary Montrose. The armored truck driver Gryms murdered in Denver," she spat.

"Small world." Dirk marched her to where his partner was dealing with their suspect. By the time they caught up, Hank had the man splayed out on the concrete and was cuffing his hands behind his back.

HANK FORCED his captive to his knees and grinned at Dirk, but his smile instantly disappeared in shock. "Linda?"

Dirk explained her connection to Gryms and took over handling the suspect allowing Hank to talk to Linda.

Hank rubbed a hand over his mouth and chin. The blocks were stacking up. "You asked me about Gryms that night. I should have known something was up."

She dropped her gaze to the asphalt. "It wasn't personal, Hank."

"How did you know we were hunting him?"

Linda rolled her shoulders back, adjusting her wrists in their metal bracelets. "I saw Cora Johnson on the news, and her situation had Gryms all over it. So, I staked out her house, hoping he'd show." She gave Hank a defiant glare. "Then you two showed up. I figured you were cops by the way you walked and how you talked to Ms. Johnson, so I followed you when you left her house."

"And then you figured you'd come on to me at the bar to get information on Gryms? You came to my room." Hank's tone was accusing, but he wasn't sure whom he blamed her or himself.

Linda shrugged but didn't answer.

"Okay, but how did you know he'd be here, today?"

"Again, the news. They report the likelihood of where he'll strike next. I've been waiting here in Bismarck for his next move and then this morning as I was getting dressed, Ms. Johnson's murder was headline news. I rushed over here right away. It was the closest I've been to catching him. I saw you and Dirk on the move and as soon as this guy took off, I knew it was him."

"Are you a police officer?" Hank took a step closer to her but stopped himself.

"No. Well, not yet." Linda scraped her booted heel on the dirt. "Probably never will be now. But the only thing that matters is that scumbag is going to jail."

"You want be a cop?"

"Yeah."

"Let me go." The cuffed man attempted to jerk away from Dirk's grasp. "I didn't do anything! What the hell, dude!"

Dirk yanked the hood from his head. "Then why were you running and shooting at us?"

"'Cuz you were chasing me, dude. I was scared for my life."

"Right," he replied, not bothering to argue with the guy. "Are you Simeon Gryms?"

"Who's asking?"

Dirk held up his badge. "Deputy US Marshal Sterling. Simeon Gryms, you are under arrest for the murders of an armored car driver in Denver and of Cora Johnson, among a laundry list of other fraudulent crimes."

Linda's mouth gaped. "You guys are marshals?

Hank squared his shoulders with pride. "Surprised?"

"Impressed." She grinned at him. "Guess that's why I couldn't get any information out of you."

Hank couldn't help the grin that spread across his mouth. It felt good to be admired for being a marshal.

Gryms sneered. "You guys don't have jurisdiction in Colorado."

"I'm a deputy US marshal, idiot." Dirk yanked Gryms to his feet. "I have jurisdiction everywhere in the United States. You're coming with us." He lifted his chin in acknowledgement at Hank. "Impressive speed, kid. Lucky for Gryms here, too. If I was alone, I'd have had to shoot him to stop him."

"You probably should have. You'd have saved the taxpayers a ton of money." Hank flashed another smile at Linda.

"Hey, you guys," Gryms whined. "I have rights."

"Yeah. You have the right to remain silent..." Dirk recited the perp's Miranda rights on their way to drop him off with the detectives in charge of the Johnson murder investigation.

"Typical arrogance of killers, showing up at the scene of the crime." The lead detective passed Gryms off to two of his officers for processing. "Arrogant and stupid. Glad you guys were on your toes out there." They exchanged contact information, and they shook hands.

"What are you going to do with me?" Linda asked Hank.

Dirk held up her gun. "I'll hang on to this for you." He turned a piercing gaze to Hank. "I'll wait for you in the car."

Ten minutes later, Hank joined him in the Explorer and barked out a laugh. "All in a morning's work, eh, Sterling?"

"Right? So, where did you leave things with Linda?"

"She swears she was just trying to get information from me about where to find Gryms and that nothing happened that night. She said she would have done anything it took, but I passed out. And I never told her anything about Gryms, either."

"You let her go?"

Hank shrugged. "You have her gun and Gryms is in custody. I don't think she's a menace to society at large, do you? Besides, she wants to be a cop. That won't happen with any of this on her record."

Dirk started the engine. "Relieved?"

"Yeah. Sort of. I still need to have an uncomfortable conversation with Amy, so..."

"Good for you, kid. Never undervalue your integrity. You'll work it out." Dirk tapped a number on his phone and it rang over the speakers in car. "Good news, Chief. Hank single handedly took Gryms down when he tried to run from the scene. He's in the custody of the Bismarck police, and we're on our way home."

"You're kidding! Well done! I can't wait to hear all about what happened. But for now, you can focus fully on Crandall. You'll get him, too, Dirk. I know you will."

"Thanks for the vote of confidence, but it will take a lot more men than just me. Hank and I are flying down on Friday to get the team organized. I'm not worried about the ATF and ICE guys, but coordinating with the Federales is always dicey."

"No FBI support?"

"Not this time. No other marshals outside of our office, either. Crandall had to have someone on the inside of one of our agencies to coordinate his escape, and I'm not taking any chances."

29

———

It had been a long but productive day. With Gryms in the bag, Emory could rest easy. Dirk and Henry won her the case that she wanted. It was late, and she was hungry but didn't feel like cooking, so she stopped by the Bison Grille to grab dinner to go. She entered the restaurant and told the hostess she was there to pick up her order. Emory sat on the bench in the lobby to wait when she noticed someone in the back of the dining room waving. Squinting, she saw it was Laurie Dillinger. When Laurie's date turned to see who she was gesturing to, Emory realized the man was Dave.

Her skin itched at the potential awkwardness of having to walk across the room to say hello. But Emory took a deep breath, squared her shoulders, and went.

"Hi Laurie. Dave. What a nice surprise seeing you both here."

Dave stood. "Emory. How are you?" He pulled out a chair for her to sit.

"Honestly," she grimaced, "I'm exhausted. It's been a

long day, but we finally caught the bad guy, so it's also been a good one."

"Are you here alone?" Dave scanned the hostess area. "Why don't you join us?"

"No, thanks. I don't want to interrupt your date. I'll go as soon as they bring me my order. How is it going with you guys?"

Laurie smiled shyly, and a beautiful rose color warmed her cheeks as she reached across the table to take Dave's hand. "We're doing well." Dave clasped her fingers in return, and they exchanged a glowing gaze before she turned to Emory. "I suppose Dirk told you that Dave and I are seeing each other."

"Yes, he mentioned it. I'm happy for you both." Which Emory was, but the obvious intimacy they shared so early in their relationship surprised her.

Dave wiped his mouth with his napkin and shifted his chair to face Emory. "Where's Sterling? I figured he would be with you."

Emory didn't want to discuss work and imagined Laurie was tired of hearing it all, anyway, so she kept her answer short. "He's on the job."

"I wondered because Laurie mentioned he might be travelling to Africa?"

Emory drew her chin in. "Africa?" She shot a questioning glance at Laurie. "No, he's in North Dakota right now. He and Henry just apprehended Simeon Gryms."

Laurie's face brightened with a smile. "Congratulations! I know you've been chasing Gryms for a while. It must feel good to bring that case to a close."

"More than you know."

Dave tilted his head. "Maybe it was Mexico? Are they planning a mission south of the border?"

Thankfully, the restaurant hostess brought Emory's order, and she avoided answering him. The woman held up a brown bag. "Do you still want to take this to go? We could plate it and bring it to the table if you'd rather?"

Emory rose and took the sack. "No, thank you. I just stopped by to say hello." She smiled at Laurie and Dave. "Have a nice dinner, you two."

Once again, Dave got to his feet. He touched her elbow. "You're welcome to stay if you like. You don't have to eat supper alone."

"No, thanks. I won't intrude on your date."

"Maybe the four of us could have dinner together sometime. When did you say Sterling was going to be out of town again?"

"I didn't." Something in Emory's gut tightened. "But I'll check our schedules and give Laurie a call. We can try to make that happen. Talk to you soon." She left the restaurant, tipping the hostess on her way out.

Emory was halfway home when her phone rang. "Hi, Mom. What's up?"

"Hello, Darling." Her mother's smooth, elegant voice echoed around the interior of the car. "Your father saw on the news that Simeon Gryms is in custody. Isn't that one of your cases?"

"Yes." Emory grinned, thrilled that her father witnessed her team's success play out on the national news. "My deputies, Sterling and Flannigan, arrested him in North Dakota just this morning."

"Oh? The broadcast didn't mention your deputies."

"They never do."

"Well, congratulations. But that's only one of the reasons I'm calling. Your father and I would like to come to Montana for a visit since it didn't work out last summer. We're thinking Thanksgiving?"

The muscles in Emory's jaw tightened. "Thanksgiving? At my apartment?"

A rustling noise echoed through the speakers of her car before her father's gruff voice reverberated against the windows. "I'm awful proud of you, Ladybug. You say that man you're seeing was the one who brought Gryms down?"

"Thanks, Daddy, and *both* Deputies Sterling and Flannigan caught him." She did not want to discuss Dirk or their relationship with her father. Scott Grey was a two-star general in the United States Marine Corps, and Dirk was a former Marine officer. Once her dad got to know Dirk, she knew he'd approve. But putting Dirk through the "getting to know the general" process would be brutal.

"Yes, Deputy Sterling. He's the one I'm talking about. You two have been dating, haven't you?"

Dating wasn't exactly how she would describe their relationship, but it suited the discussion. "Yes, sir."

"Right. Then, it's time your mother and I met him. We'll arrive in Billings the Tuesday before Thanksgiving and stay through Sunday. Your mother will let you know the flight details as soon as we have them." Her father did not ask, he commanded.

"I think I can make that work. But I don't know what Dirk has planned. There's no guarantee you'll get to meet him while you're here." Emory turned into the parking lot of her apartment building and slid into her reserved spot.

"He'll make himself available if he wants to make a good impression."

"Daddy, please. We are grown adults with lives of our own. Just because he was in the Marine Corps does not mean you can order him around."

"Perhaps. But the fact that you're my daughter, does. Is that clear?"

"Yes, sir." She sighed. Here she was, in her late thirties, instantly feeling like a child under her father's authority. She couldn't imagine *that* going over very well with Dirk. But she supposed it was time to find out. "Unless he's traveling on an open case, I'm sure he'll do his best to be there."

"Very good. Congratulations again, Ladybug. This gives me bragging rights at the Pentagon. Your mother will get back to you soon." The call ended. Her father was not one for idle chitchat.

Emory gathered her purse along with her dinner and climbed the stairs to her apartment. She kicked off her shoes and warmed the food in the microwave while she called Dirk.

"Hi. This is a pleasant surprise. I didn't expect to hear from you again tonight." Dirk's rough voice curled inside her like smoke. "Everything okay?"

"Well, I won't see you until after you get back from the mission in Mexico, and I had a few things I wanted to tell you. First, you'll never guess who I ran into when I picked up my dinner."

"Can't imagine."

"Laurie Dillinger and Dave Aldrich."

Dirk groaned. "I guess I better get used to them as a couple. Billings is still a small town."

"Yes, it is." Emory sat at the table with her meal. "For some odd reason, Dave thought you were in Africa. That's strange, isn't it?"

Dirk was silent for a moment. "I mentioned something about Africa to Laurie, but nothing about going there. He's probably just digging to see what we're up to. You know, the FBI is always a step behind the Marshals. Always trying to catch up." His warm laugh settled her nerves.

"You're probably right. The other reason I called is my parents are coming to Montana for Thanksgiving and... I'm afraid dinner is a command performance—front and center—for you."

Dirk chuckled. "A direct order from the two-star, huh?"

Emory sighed. "That's exactly what it is. I'm sorry."

"Don't worry about it, Em. He's not the first general I've stood tall in front of. And as your dad, he is entitled."

30

Dirk and Hank slept on the all-nighter to Mexico City so they would arrive fully rested for their morning meeting with the team gathered together to take down Beaux Crandall. The plan was to arrest him the minute he stepped onto Mexican soil. Agents from ATF and ICE and a dozen Federales met inside the Policia Federal hangar at Mexico City's Benito Juárez International Airport.

They spent the day practicing and refining their snatch-and-grab strategy. They did not know how many bodyguards Crandall had with him, so they guessed a minimum of two, along with two pilots. Presumably, all passengers on the jet carried guns. They expected a driver to collect Crandall and assumed he, too, would have a weapon.

Dirk addressed the team. "It's imperative we remain out of sight until Crandall's feet touch the ground. We must wait for him to get off the plane. If he catches our scent before then, he can easily turn the jet and take off.

We'll have missed our opportunity and won't likely get another. Ideally, we grab him in the open space between the hangar and his car. That way, we can maintain cover while he and his men are exposed."

Hank concluded the mission plan. "If everything goes smoothly, we'll have Crandall surrounded and can take him and everyone with him into custody with no shots fired. ICE is assisting us with his extradition and is flying us home on an MD80. We'll immediately fly Crandall to the US before anyone is even aware he touched down in Mexico."

Crandall's pilot posted a last-minute flight plan into Mexico City and the jet's scheduled arrival time was 6:14 pm. The cross-agency law enforcement teams hid in various locations, ready and waiting for Crandall's jet to land. At 6:05 pm, a black town car glided across the tarmac and parked, with the engine running, approximately forty feet from the hangar slated to house Crandall's aircraft.

Dirk spoke in hushed tones over the radio. "Remember, we do not know who, or how many people are in that limo. We must grab Crandall before he gets to that car but watch your six."

Air traffic control reported the moment Crandall's jet entered Benito Juárez International Airport's controlled airspace. The team maintained their cover as they watched the sporty plane land and waited motionless as it taxied into the private hangar. The agents held a collective breath, waiting for Crandall to emerge from the building and walk to the car standing by.

Without warning, a powerful engine growled and

tires squealed on the pavement. Before anyone on the team registered what happened, a sleek, black four-door Alpha Romeo catapulted from the back doors of the hangar.

Someone yelled, "He's getting away!"

Dirk didn't hesitate. He shouted to Hank, "Come on, kid!" They raced to a black-and-gold Federales Charger and jumped in. Hank waved at the surprised Federales who stood with their guns drawn, staring at the taillights of the Alpha Romeo escaping into the burgeoning dusk. Dirk revved the powerful Charger's engine once, then threw it into gear.

Flooring it, he made a tight, squealing turn. Smoke from the tires clouded the sky. The smell of burnt rubber singed Dirk's throat. He tasted its bitterness on his tongue as they took off after the runaway car. Shots flew at them from the sports vehicle ahead and Crandall who was sitting in the back, peered at them from the rear window. Dirk sped to catch them while Hank fired back.

"Where did that car come from?" Hank strapped the belt tight across his chest. "I didn't see it in the hangar earlier."

Dirk skidded around a corner, chasing after Crandall, fury fueling his need for speed. "Don't know. But they obviously knew we were there. They had a plan."

"Where's my rifle when I need it?"

"Let me get you closer." Dirk shifted, and the Charger surged forward.

Together, the cars screamed down the highway that circled the city. Dirk gained on them, but then they shot across three lanes of traffic to exit onto de la Reforma.

"They're headed into the city center!" Hank yelled their location into the radio.

"Don't lose them!" came the reply.

Dirk swerved to miss the four cars that had crashed into each other, trying to avoid the careening Alfa Romeo. The glossy black bullet slammed on its brakes, barely making the turn onto Eje Central Lázaro Cárdenas. Hot on their tale, the Charger blazed past the beautifully lit Oalacio de Bellas Artes building with its glowing golden domes.

Hank smacked the dash. "Here we are in Mexico City again, and I *still* don't have time to visit the art museum."

Dirk grinned and pulled the emergency brake, forcing a sliding turn onto the road next to the museum. "This street is one way going the other way. Hold on!" He dodged the oncoming traffic like he was in a life and death game of Frogger at Mach 9.

Up ahead, Crandall's escape vehicle grazed the nose of a car entering the intersection, causing it to flip. The old Subaru bounced on its side and rolled to the roof directly in Dirk's path. He yanked the wheel and missed the sedan with its upside-down passengers by a breath, but the Federales behind them weren't so lucky. More Federales in a truck fitted with a machine gun mounted on the cab instantly replaced them. They surged into their compatriot's position.

As soon as Dirk made it through the next intersection, a semi-truck carrying a load of five-gallon water bottles entered the crossing lane. The Federales didn't react in time. They slammed into the bed of the truck, sending plastic bottles and an explosion of water everywhere.

Behind him, Dirk caught glimpses of the crashes in his rearview mirror. "Where are the ATF guys? These Federales don't know how to drive." His pulse hummed in concert with the engine. He returned his eagle-like focus to the road just in time to swerve, barely missing a group of tourists stepping off the sidewalk. "Holy hell!"

The evasive maneuver cost him time, and the Alfa Romeo gained ground. Dirk jammed his foot on the gas. Crandall's car sped through an intersection and skidded into a turn. They raced back onto the freeway.

Cars slammed on their brakes and honked angry horns. Dirk followed as fast as he could without causing more accidents. Another chase vehicle couldn't make the turn, and it slid sideways into the traffic-light. The electrical structure fell and shattered on the pavement below.

Dirk gunned the Charger as he sped into the darkening night. On the radio, Hank yelled they were leaving the city. A crackling voice replied. "Are you still on Highway 95D?"

"Yes. Headed southwest with our hair on fire. Any ideas of where Crandall is going? Is there another airport out here?"

"No, not for miles. But there is the Rancho de Castilla."

"Why would he want to go there?"

The radio operator paused a second too long, and Dirk's gut clamped down. "It is the home of Reynaldos Castilla, head of one of the fiercest cartels in Mexico City."

Hank pressed the button on the side of the mic. "Do you think Crandall knows the guy? Could he seek refuge on his ranch?"

"I'm saying that if you don't catch him before he gets there, you never will. We can't match the firepower Heffe Castilla has, and we won't back you if you try."

The Alfa Romeo slowed slightly to exit the highway once again. Dirk followed without slowing. The sports car paused at the bottom of the ramp, turning right. Dirk pushed their vehicle even harder. The Charger jumped the curb and, catching air, left the road. They flew through the air and crash-landed, smashing into the left front corner panel of the beautiful Italian car.

Pushing past the deployed airbag, Dirk leapt from the car. He ignored the searing pain in his chest and ran to the Alpha Romeo before the man sitting shotgun could raise his weapon. Hank yanked open the passenger door and fired, hitting the gunslinger in the head. Dirk aimed his gun at the driver. "Don't move!"

Hank toe-heeled backward to the rear door. He pulled it open and found Crandall balled up on the floor, trembling with fear. "Gotcha, you son of a bitch!"

Seconds later, by the time ATF, ICE, and the few remaining Federales vehicles squealed to a stop around them, Dirk and Hank had the driver and Beaux Crandall handcuffed and on their knees.

Hank grinned at Dirk. "Book 'em, Danno."

31

———

Sitting on either side of Crandall, Hank and Dirk rode back to the city in a Federale SUV. They escorted their prisoner all the way to a jail guarded by ATF agents. Garcia, Dirk's ATF buddy, promised to stand guard personally over Crandall while EMTs checked Dirk and Hank for injury.

Dirk was reluctant to leave. "Don't let him out of your sight, Garcia. Not even to take a piss."

"I got this." The agent looked like he'd fit right in with the drug pushers on the streets of Mexico City.

Hank gripped Dirk's shoulder. "Come on, Sterling. Crandall is in safe hands, and you need to get your ribs checked out."

Dirk glared at him. "I'm fine. Besides, they can't do anything for cracked ribs, anyway."

"Maybe not, but let's go make sure there isn't a break threatening to puncture a lung. I don't want to have to be the one to tell the chief you died of neglect."

"Yeah, yeah." Dirk glanced back at Garcia. "Stay alert. This sleaze has resources. He's escaped before."

At the hospital, a nurse cleaned their cuts and scrapes. She gave Hank three stitches to close a cut on his forehead and sent him to wait for Dirk. They sent his partner to radiology to x-ray his ribs while Hank went in search of food. The excitement of the chase left him famished.

Finally, an orderly wheeled Dirk out to the waiting room in a chair. Hank smirked at the pissed-off look on his partner's bruised face. "All good?"

"Let's get out of here." Dirk pushed himself out of the wheelchair. He grimaced, and he held his rib cage.

The orderly frowned. "Señor Sterling has two cracked ribs. The doctor taped them, but he needs to rest until they heal."

"Right." Hank didn't bother assuring the man. Dirk would gut it out, no matter what the doctor said. "I grabbed a protein bar from a vending machine, but I'm still starving. Let's get some food."

Hank tried to help Dirk get into the car, but his partner brushed the attempt away. They had a borrowed ATF vehicle for use until their flight back to the states the next day, and Hank drove to the nearest cantina that was still open that late and served food.

Dirk grunted as he climbed out of the car. "Do you find it ironic that the only injuries we have came from the airbags that are supposed to protect us?"

Hank held the bar door open for Dirk. "Yeah, but if they didn't deploy, we'd both be in far worse condition.

Those ribs would have broken, and that might be the least of the problems."

"I guess."

They sat at the bar and ordered platters of Birria with extra tortillas and beer. Hank poked at the sauce laden meat with his fork. "Beef or... what kind of meat is this?"

"Either beef or goat. Who cares?" Dirk dug in. "I could eat two goats all by myself, right now."

Hank agreed, and when he tasted the savory dish, he couldn't eat it fast enough. The crash of blood sugar, adrenaline, and cortisol after their chase left him seriously depleted. "Are we going to see Maria Cortez before we leave tomorrow?"

"I'd like to. Without her, we might never have got our hands on Crandall."

"I'll call Teresa in the morning and get her working on Maria's reward."

"Good. She deserves it."

ON THE WAY to Maria's the next morning, Hank stopped at a local market to get Maria a gift. They drove through the city, noticing workers still cleaning up messes caused by their car chase from the night before.

Hank slowed as they rolled past the art museum. "This is the third time we've gone by this place, and I *still* don't have time to go in."

"This isn't the Navy, kid. The USMS never promised you would 'See the World'. Besides, when did you become an art aficionado?"

"I'm not. But it seems like a sign. I keep driving by but

can't go in." Hank wasn't sure why it bothered him, but he didn't have time to think it through.

Maria was sitting in the morning sunshine in her courtyard, weaving another basket, when they pulled up. She smiled and her whole body seemed to nod when they walked toward her.

"Buenos días, Maria." Dirk reached for her hand.

"So, you caught him?"

"We did. Thanks to you. And I heard from a friend of mine in Interpol, they've found his island compound and are tending to his victims. Soon, the authorities will help the women and children Crandall kept as slaves get back home. Think of all the families you helped to give indescribable joy."

"I know what it's like to have a child stolen from you. To not know where he is or if he's dead or alive." Maria's eyes clouded over.

Hank squatted down and handed her his gift, wrapped in a brown paper bag. "This is for you. It's not much, but..." Maria opened the paper and pulled out a beautiful hand-carved picture frame. "I thought you might like to put a picture of your son in it."

Maria reached her hand to his face and touched his cheek. "You are a good boy. I will treasure your gift."

"Our office is processing the paperwork for your reward. The money coming to you will keep you in comfort, but if you ever need anything. Please let us know."

"Thank you, both. I want to apologize for the crimes of my son. If only things were different."

Dirk cleared his throat, likely trying to cover for the

emotion stamped all over his face. "You've redeemed that evil, Maria. Without your help, hundreds of people would have remained in slavery. Now hundreds of families are reunited. They, and we, are in your debt."

Maria offered to feed them a meal, but they declined. Dirk was eager to get back to Crandall and get on their flight to Colorado.

Hank drove to the ATF headquarters feeling on top of the world. "I'd say we've had a couple of great days. We should celebrate when we get home."

"Absolutely. Once Crandall is in a cell in the Supermax, I'll party all day."

Hank wouldn't have believed anything could wreck his mood until his phone buzzed with a text from Amy.

32

———————

Dirk and Hank sat with Beaux Crandall in cuffs between them on an ICE MD80 bound for Peterson Air Force Base in Colorado Springs. Dirk insisted on escorting the dirtbag all the way to his jail cell at the federal Supermax in Florence, Colorado.

"A friend of mine in Interpol told me the authorities found your mansion in Cabo Verde. And I know you'll be glad to hear that they're returning all the men, women, and children you abducted and forced into slavery to their various homes and families. The Cabo Verde government froze all your off-shore accounts and confiscated your estate along with all your belongings, including your yacht, and has put it all up for auction. Much of the proceeds will go to enhance the lives of your victims."

Crandall laughed. "Believe that if you want to, Sterling. But I have more influence than you know. Plenty of high profile political and business figures will step in to protect my investments, lest their participation on my island be made public. You see, I'm completely protected. I may spend a few uncomfortable days in jail, but believe me, I won't be there for long."

"That's where you're wrong, Crandall. You slithered away once before, but it won't happen again."

"Tell me, Sterling, how did you know I was flying into Mexico City?"

"I know everything," Dirk murmured. He would never tell Crandall that Maria was the one who sold him out. "Who tipped you off that we were there waiting for you to land at the airport?"

Crandall released a wheezy laugh that culminated in a coughing fit. When he regained his breath, he said, "I have friends in federal places. Don't you know the FBI and me are like this?" He crossed his fat fingers to showing how tight he thought he was with the Agency. "You never know who you can trust or who might put your friends and loved ones in danger."

A sick knowing washed through Dirk's body. Crandall wasn't just blowing smoke. Everything clicked together in Dirk's mind. The leak *was* from the FBI and the mole was David Aldrich. It had to be. Why else had he been keeping tabs on Dirk's movements, first through Emory and then through Laurie? How else could Crandall know about the trap set in Mexico? It had to be Aldrich who tipped him off. Thinking about Dave Aldrich anywhere near Laurie and Caleb Dillinger made his skin crawl. He swore to protect them, but he'd ended up bringing a jackal into their lives.

Hank wasn't listening to the conversation. He sat next to the window, distracted by his phone. His fingers flew over the screen as he texted. Crandall adjusted his girth in the seat and leaned his head back. He drifted to sleep, snoring loudly.

No less exhausted than his captive, Dirk elbowed Crandall's bloated belly. "Wake up. This isn't a luxury trip." Dirk wasn't about to listen to the man buzz-saw all the way to Colorado. He studied his partner's hunched frame. Something was wrong, but he didn't want to ask him about it in front of Crandall.

After they landed, the plane taxied to the hangar at Peterson Airfield, where a combined team of US Marshals, MPs, and State Police met them at the bottom of the steps. The state cops transferred Crandall to a paneled van inside which they cuffed his ankles to a chain attached to the floor, and his wrists to the metal bench.

Five cars drove in a line off the base and onto the highway. The convoy consisted of a State Patrol car, followed by a US Marshals vehicle and the prisoner's van. Behind them was a second Marshals SUV carrying Dirk and Hank. Bringing up the end was a final State Patrol cruiser. All eyes watched for signs of ambush.

Forty-five minutes later, the procession entered the first gate on the secured grounds of the Supermax prison. They allowed only the armor-plated van and the marshal's SUV through the second gate. They stopped at the prison's entrance check point.

Crandall had already been sentenced to life in prison and so, though he had more trials to attend, he would wait them out in an isolated jail cell. True to his word, Dirk followed Crandall through every step of his intake processing, including the blubbery man's cavity search. He walked a step behind him through the gen pop that smelled of weak disinfectant, hugely overwhelmed by masculine BO.

Dirk didn't take his eyes off his prisoner until the jail cell slammed shut behind him with a satisfying bang. The mechanical sound of the lock on the heavy door set something free in Dirk's chest. His breath came full and easy for the first time in months.

"Good luck in here, Crandall. I hear child molesters do really well in prison." Dirk turned on his heel and left Crandall behind bars where he belonged. Secretly, he hoped the other prisoners would give Crandall his due for the crimes he committed against innocence.

Hank waited for him where they had separated at intake. "Locked up safe and sound?"

"I wish they'd throw away the key. I hate the thought that my tax dollars are helping to feed that pig." Dirk clapped Hank on the shoulder as they turned to leave. On the way out of the Supermax, they retrieved their weapons and other personal items not allowed inside the prison. A lone US Marshal vehicle waited for them outside the last gate to take them back to the base.

Dirk and Hank debriefed their mission while grabbing a quick bite of pizza at a place in the PX. He told Hank that Garcia explained why the ATF and ICE guys didn't join the car chase the night before. "They stayed at the airport to deal with Crandall's small army of guards. Garcia said he figured as invested as Dirk was, they knew he'd catch his man with back-up from the Federales."

Hank swallowed a huge bite. "I still want to know where that Alpha Romeo came from."

"Apparently, Crandall kept it hidden behind a false wall in the hangar, ready for situations like last night. If we hadn't acted as fast as we did by jumping in that Charger, Crandall would be in the wind again."

Dirk and Hank walked to the flight line and waited in the ready room for the chief pilot's final approval for their ride home. Hank continued his obsession with his phone and Dirk nudged his shoulder. "Have you been talking to Amy all this time?" Dirk stretched out his legs and shifted to ease the stress on his ribs.

"Yeah. One minute she wants me to move home, the next she's not sure if she ever wants to see me again. When she found out we were coming home from Mexico, she lost it." Hank tucked his phone into his back pocket. "I don't know what to do. I don't even know how I feel anymore. There was a time I would have done anything to make it work, but I'm tired of the constant emotional turmoil. I don't think a career as a deputy marshal is conducive to family life." He propped his elbows on his knees and buried his face in his hands.

"Plenty of families make it work." Dirk was concerned about his partner. They had just come through an extremely stressful situation. His own adrenaline and cortisol levels were finally fully draining from his system, leaving him exhausted. He figured the same was true for Hank, and now the kid had to deal with his distraught wife, too. Dirk had no advice to give, and he didn't share his thoughts about Aldrich. No sense in adding more to Hank's already overflowing plate.

"If it weren't for the baby, the decision wouldn't be as difficult. Of course, I can't deny that some of Amy's instability probably comes from the pregnancy hormones. That's not her fault, but it's hard to separate her body chemistry from her emotional explosions."

Dirk kept his eyes closed but offered his thoughts. "So, maybe you hang on until after the baby is born and see if things get back to normal."

"Yeah. But it might be best if we stay separated until then. Amy says she misses me and that she's miserable without me, but she's even more miserable when I'm home. With as much as we've been traveling, she'd have blown a gasket if I was living with her."

"I bet the chief would give you time off to go to Amy's doctor's appointments. You don't want to miss watching the baby grow and hearing its heartbeat." Dirk was walking very close to a painful line he didn't like to visit. All his memories of his ex-wife, Hannah's, pregnancy and their young son, Bennett's, brief life pierced his heart and made it hard to breathe.

"You're right about that. I want to be there for every part of my little guy's life. But I should probably start looking for an apartment. I can't stay at your place forever."

"It's not a problem, kid. I'm over at Emory's a lot, anyway. Besides, I know how much you make." Dirk peeked at his partner through mostly closed eyes.

Hank hung his head. "Thanks man. I appreciate it."

"You got it—but you owe me." Dirk curled the side of his mouth in a lopsided grin when Hank turned to look at him. "You have to come with me to Emory's for

Thanksgiving. Your job will be to act as a buffer between me and her overly protective, two-star general of a father."

Hank chuffed. "Done."

Dirk reached for his phone to text Emory: **It's over. We've locked Crandall away for good.**

Emory: **Congratulations! I can't wait to celebrate with you!**

Dirk: **Me too. Hey, do me a favor?**

Emory: **Anything, Superman.**

Dirk: **Check on Laurie. I've been putting the pieces together and I think Aldrich is the mole.**

Emory: **What makes you think that?**

Dirk: **I'll fill you in when I get home. I'll meet you at Laurie's. Stay with her until I get back to Billings.**

Emory: **Okay. See you there.**

33

———

Emory prepared to leave the office and drive over to Laurie Dillinger's house. She considered asking Teresa to go with her, but Teresa had plans with Tomas after work and Emory didn't want to mess that up. It was good to see Teresa taking time to enjoy life and not just be a slave to it. Emory tried to picture what it would be like to have children—to have a family to come home to at the end of the day. People whom she loved, and who relied on her. She had made career choices that didn't allow time for a marriage, let alone babies. But now that she had become a Chief Deputy, was it too late?

Brushing away what could have been, and the strange sense of missing people who didn't exist, Emory opened Sam Dillinger's old employee file to get Laurie's home address. She had never been there before and needed directions. Google Maps told her the house was twenty minutes away.

She stopped at Teresa's desk on her way out. "I'm

leaving for the night. Why don't you close up shop and get out of here too?"

"I will as soon as I confirm the FBI has all the information they need to disburse the reward money to Maria Cortez for her help in catching Crandall."

"Listen, I know you have plans with your son tonight, but let's grab a drink after work sometime."

Teresa's gaze shifted from her computer screen to Emory. She studied her for a few seconds before smiling. "I'd like that."

Emory rested her hand on Teresa's shoulder. "Good. I would too. See you in the morning."

"Good night."

On her way to Laurie's house, Emory ran through several possible excuses for randomly stopping by. She could pretend that she was in the neighborhood, or that after seeing Laurie and Dave at the restaurant the other night, she thought it might be fun to stop by. Nothing she came up with sounded believable.

Apprehension jittered its way up Emory's spine when she turned the corner on to Laurie's street and saw Dave's car sitting in front of the woman's house. She should have known he'd be there. He was always slightly obsessive—verging on possessive and controlling—when she had dated him. It was one reason things didn't work out between them. Her feelings for Dirk were the other.

Emory drew in a breath and parked behind Dave's car. She walked across the lawn, climbed the steps to the front porch, and knocked.

Seconds later, Laurie opened the door. Her face held surprise. "Hi, Emory. What are you doing here?" Her gaze shifted to the yard beyond Emory. "Is Dirk with you?" Her eyes snapped back to Emory's face and her smile faded. Fear filled her eyes and stretched her expression into one of worry. "Did something happen? Is Dirk... is he alright?"

Too late, Emory realized that her sudden appearance on Laurie's doorstep would frighten her. She had experienced her husband's chief arriving unexpectedly on her doorstep the day she lost Sam to the job. Emory reached a hand forward, touching the screen that stood between them. "No, Laurie! I'm sorry to scare you. Dirk is fine. He's good. In fact, he and Henry are on their way home tonight. I just dropped by to say hello."

Laurie's brows dipped together in confusion. Not surprising, since Emory had never stopped by for any reason before. "Okay... Well, that's a relief. Come on in." Laurie opened the screen door, and Emory stepped inside the cute little house. "Dave is here, too. We just started a fire and poured some wine. Can I get you a glass?"

On a normal day, Emory would immediately decline and leave the couple to themselves, but nothing about this day was normal and Dirk had asked her to keep an eye on his friend. "Sure. I'd love one, thank you." She followed Laurie into the kitchen.

"Dave, look who's here."

Dave was bent over with his head in the refrigerator, and he stood. A flash of what Emory read as pure anger sparked in his eyes a mere second before it disappeared. He replaced the expression with a well-practiced smile. "Emory, what a surprise."

"Hi Dave. I just stopped by to say hello. I had such a pleasant time with you two at the restaurant the other night. And I thought it would be nice to get to know Laurie a little better. What have you guys been up to?" Emory accepted a glass of red wine from Laurie.

Dave tossed a packet of cheese slices on the counter. "We've been spending a lot of time with Caleb. Tonight, we were hoping to get some alone time." He sliced coins of summer sausage and set them on a plate. "You know, Emory, it's strange. I never see you around town and yet in the last two days, I've seen you twice."

"Yes, odd coincidence, isn't it?" The little hairs covering Emory's skin stirred. Dave was clearly unhappy that she was there. She glanced about the kitchen and living room. "Where is Caleb, by the way?"

Laurie finished lining up the cheese slices on the plate and pulled a box of crackers from the cupboard. "He and Bear are playing in his room. Caleb's giving up naps, but Mommy still needs the quiet time." Smiling, she winked at Dave.

Dave lifted the dish and pushed by Emory on his way to the living room. "Yeah, it's hard to get adult time together."

His waspish tone clearly showed how he felt about Emory's sudden appearance. She was obviously interrupting their cozy time in front of the fire. But in case what Dirk suspected was true, Emory wasn't going anywhere. She had promised to check on Laurie and stay until Dirk got there. And that was exactly what she was going to do. Emory carried a small basket filled with crackers and followed Laurie into the living room with a bottle of wine and a bowl of apple slices.

"This is really nice." Emory took a seat in a side chair next to the sofa. Laurie sat next to Dave on the couch, tucking her feet underneath her. Emory sipped her wine. "Thanks for including me."

Laurie glanced at Dave, but he was staring hard at Emory. "Of course. You're welcome anytime."

Emory glanced at her watch. "I won't stay long, but this is a real treat. I wasn't looking forward to another night eating dinner by myself." Dirk should be there within the hour. She'd have to keep up her friendly façade until then. "I'm grateful for the company. It's too quiet when Dirk and Hank are out of town."

"As I recall, you always told me you enjoyed having time to yourself," Dave challenged. "In fact, you said you *needed* it. Wasn't that why you never wanted me to come over on Saturday afternoons when we were dating?"

"That's all water under the bridge now, Dave. Don't you think? You and Laurie seem happy spending long days together." Emory searched for something to say that would change the subject. She wasn't about to rehash their poor attempt at a relationship in front of Laurie. "Is Caleb in pre-school this year?"

Laurie smiled with relief. "Yes. Just two half days a week at the church down the road. But he loves it. The only thing he'd like better would be if he could bring Bear with him."

"I bet. And I'm sure it gives you some time to yourself to run errands and things."

"Yes. I'm using the time to restart my graphic design business."

"That's exciting, Laurie." Emory was genuinely happy for her. "Does Dirk know? He'll be so pleased for you. What type of design do you do?"

Laurie explained the work she had done before Caleb was born. "I need to take a few classes to get up to date with all the new technology, but then I should be able to run with it." She beamed with excitement and kept the conversation going by sharing her dreams. When she'd exhausted that topic, she went on about how Caleb was doing in school, the new friends he had made, and his silly antics with his dog.

A dark energy vibrated off Dave as he stared at Emory with barely restrained hostility. He didn't bother trying to mask his feelings. Wondering at his agitated reaction to her presence, Emory pretended to be oblivious to his mood. She laughed at Laurie's stories and asked questions to keep her talking.

As the dinner hour neared, the conversation thinned, and long moments of uncomfortable silence punctuated their visit. Emory glanced once again at her watch. Where was Dirk? She couldn't keep this up for much longer. Dave was already suspicious, and it was only a matter of time before he showed her the door.

Dave drained his glass. "Late for something?"

Emory startled. "No. I was just checking the time out of habit."

"It's getting close to the dinner hour. I'm sure you have plans. Aren't you meeting Sterling or someone?" Dave's glare confronted her.

"Nope," she flapped a hand at him. "He's out of town. I'm on my own, tonight."

Laurie glanced hesitantly at Dave before she politely invited Emory to stay. "Why don't you join us for dinner? It's only spaghetti and meatballs, but there's plenty."

"Thank you. You're so kind. I'd love to." Emory eased back into her chair, but Dave shot out of his.

"I'm gonna check on Caleb," he grumbled and strode down the hall.

"Is there anything I can do to help you in the kitchen?" Emory asked Laurie, keeping her tone light, but her gaze shot to the dark hallway when she heard a bedroom door slam.

Laurie set her to the task of chopping lettuce. She tossed it with tomatoes, carrots, and celery in a large bowl when the door slammed again. Emory looked up in time to see Dave give Caleb a shove to hurry him into the living room. Laurie stopped slicing bread and faced Dave. Confusion and anger clouded her face.

"What's going on?" Laurie darted a concerned gaze over her son.

The atmosphere was thick, stirring Emory's sense of pending danger. She edged to the side of the table, prepared for anything.

Caleb's lower lip trembled, and he ran to his mother, throwing his arms around her waist. "Mommy, Mr. Dave pushed me."

Laurie scooted Caleb behind her so that she stood between her son and Dave. "Dave? What happened?"

Emory's pulse rose in anticipation, and she crossed

her arms to hide her fingers inching toward the Glock she carried in a shoulder holster under her blazer.

But Dave, a highly trained agent, was faster. He already had his gun in hand, and he pointed it at Laurie. "Don't try it, Emory, or I'll shoot her. Slowly remove your weapon and toss it on the floor behind me. Don't try anything stupid, either. Too many people here will lose, and none of them will be me."

Emory's heart clamored so hard it punched holes in her breath. She did as Dave ordered, tossing her gun onto the carpet. She had a second weapon nestled at the small of her back and watched for an opportunity to reach for it. "What are you doing, Dave?" She tried to distract him. "What is this all about?"

"How stupid do you think I am, Emory? You and Laurie aren't friends. Not the kind that drop by unexpectedly in the middle of the afternoon and never leave. Why are you here?"

Laurie's voice trembled on the edge of hysteria. "Dave, what are you doing? What's going on?" Her eyes darted between Dave and Emory. "Why were you angry with Caleb and are you pointing your gun at me?"

In the room down the hall, Bear barked frantically. He scratched wildly at the door. Emory spoke over the noise in as calm a voice as she could muster. "What do you hope to gain here, Dave? What is your end goal?"

Dave grabbed Laurie's arm and yanked her toward him. Caleb fell to the floor and burst into tears when Dave held his gun to Laurie's temple. Hearing Caleb cry, Bear went ballistic, throwing his body at the door and clawing desperately. Emory hoped the dog would eventually break through the thin door. It would provide her with the distraction she needed to get her spare gun.

"Obviously, you know more than you're letting on," Dave spat. "What was your plan in coming here today? Were you waiting for an opportunity to take me unaware?" He scoffed derisively. "How did that work out for you, *Chief Grey*?"

"I'm not sure what you're talking about, Dave. But right now, all I want is to keep Laurie and Caleb safe. Whatever is going on with you doesn't involve them. Let them go, and you and I can talk."

"Not a chance. These two are my ticket out of here. You, however, are in my way." Dave rotated the muzzle of his gun and aimed it at Emory.

34

———————

Dirk shared his suspicions about Dave Aldrich with Hank on their flight home. As soon as the Air Force plane landed, they ran to their cars and Dirk told Hank to follow him. They drove straight to Laurie's. It was dark by the time Dirk turned onto her street, but in the light of a streetlamp, he saw both Emory's and Aldrich's cars parked in front of the house.

To maintain the element of surprise, Dirk left his Jeep a block away, and Hank pulled in behind him. Together, they approached the Dillinger home on foot, staying in the shadows of the houses along the way. As they neared the Dillingers' front lawn, Dirk heard Bear barking and growling frantically. Something was terribly wrong.

The men crept to Caleb's window and peered in. He saw Bear locked inside the room, clawing at the door to get out. Aldrich's voice came from the front of the house in angry shouts. Dirk grew cold, but with his fear came a crystalline focus.

He whispered to Hank. "I'll enter the house through this bedroom. I don't know how Caleb's Rottweiler will respond to you breaking in, so you go to the front door and wait for my signal." Hank gave him a nod and crouching low, crept toward the porch.

Dirk pried open Caleb's bedroom window with the blade of a knife he wore on his belt. Inside the room, Bear turned at the sound and lunged in Dirk's direction, his gleaming fangs dripping with fury. Seeing that it was Dirk, the tone of Bear's barking rose in earnest. He dashed back to the door as if telling Dirk to hurry. When Dirk got the casing fully open, he hoisted himself over the ledge and eased himself onto Caleb's bed. "Why are you locked in here?" Dirk asked the dog, though he wasn't sure he wanted the answer.

Dirk moved to the bedroom door, crunching Legos along the way. He opened it a crack to peek out and see what he was dealing with, but Bear rammed his nose into the slit and forced his way through. He bolted down the hallway.

Gripping his gun, Dirk ran after the dog toward the living room. Aldrich was so intent on threatening Emory, he didn't notice the black and tan missile spearing toward him. When he saw Bear leap, it was too late. The Rottweiler's powerful jaws clamped down on Aldrich's gun arm with over three-hundred pounds of pressure per square inch and crushed his wrist. The dog's weight and momentum knocked Aldrich to the floor, and his weapon clattered across the kitchen tiles. Unlike a trained police dog, Bear worked on instinct alone and did not stop at holding the man down. He ground his teeth and tore at Dave's shattered arm.

Emory dashed to recover the loose weapon, while Laurie pulled Caleb tight into her arms, burying his face against her legs. Hank burst through the front door and grabbed Emory's gun from the floor while Aldrich screamed in agony. Bear's bite splintered bones and ripped the FBI agent's shredded muscles from his tendons. Dirk pulled the dog off and handcuffed Dave's wrists behind his back, ignoring his cries of pain, while Emory called 911. Bear bounded to Caleb and Laurie's side, slathering the boy with worried licks.

"I always knew there was something off about you, Aldrich," Dirk growled. He left him face down on the floor. "But I had no proof. You might have gotten away with being a traitor, too, if you hadn't tried to hurt the people I care about. I can't believe you chose Crandall over the Agency. Are you into the same sick shit he's into?"

Emory held Aldrich at gunpoint while Dirk secured him. "You helped Crandall escape from prison and cost the lives of several good men. I have never been more disgusted with anyone in my whole life."

"He was blackmailing me, Em," Aldrich appealed to her. "I don't expect you to understand."

"Don't call me that. We are not friends. It makes me ill to think what you did that Crandall could use to blackmail you with."

Laurie stood with her arms around Caleb, shaking her head in bewilderment. "This whole time you were just using me to get to Dirk?"

Dave sneered. "Don't take it personally, sweetheart. Besides, you enjoyed yourself while it lasted."

A desperate cry escaped Laurie's throat, and she grasped Caleb's hand and ran down the hall to her bedroom, slamming the door behind her.

Dirk ground his knee into Aldrich's torn arm, causing him to cry out. "You're gonna pay for that, scumbag."

35

Dirk remained by Laurie's side while the police investigators took over her house. An ambulance drove Aldrich to the hospital under guard while FBI agents interviewed Laurie and Caleb. Hank left after giving his statement, but Emory stayed another hour.

Before she went home, Emory gave Laurie a hug. "If you need anything, even if you just want to grab a cup of coffee sometime, call me. Promise?"

"Thanks, Emory. This is the second time you've saved me from my own stupidity. I'll never forget it."

"Hey, you are not stupid. Aldrich is a snake who had everyone fooled except for Dirk. You're a smart and brave woman who I'd be proud to call my friend." The women embraced.

Dirk walked Emory to the door. "I'll be over as soon as Laurie feels safe on her own. It might not be until daylight."

"Take your time. I don't expect you in the office tomorrow. You or Hank. You both deserve the day off."

He drew her tight to his chest and kissed the top of her head. "Thanks for being here tonight, Em. Aldrich knew his time was short. There's no telling what he planned to do to Laurie and Caleb if you hadn't shown up."

"Of course, but it was you who saved the day."

He chuckled. "No, it was Bear." He kissed her softly and watched her until he knew she had safely locked her car.

Dirk finally left Laurie and Caleb at seven o'clock the next morning. They were curled up on her bed sleeping, with Bear standing guard. Emory would already be at the office, so he drove to his house. Hank was there, crashed out on the guest bed, so Dirk closed the shades in his room and fell onto his own bed.

Hours later, a familiar ringtone brought him back from the land of the dead. It was Emory. "Hi. Did I wake you?"

"Yeah." His voice was gravely with sleep. "But I need to get up or I won't sleep tonight."

"That sounds promising."

He chuckled. "What's up?"

"I just received a call from the Bismarck Police Department in North Dakota. They are extraditing Simeon Gryms to Colorado to face the charges for murder and armed robbery down there. The police chief wanted to know if the deputies who caught Gryms would escort him to Denver. Normally, I'd send you with Henry, but I thought maybe it would be fun if you and *I* did it together. I haven't worked outside the office for far too long."

Dirk padded into the bathroom. He scratched his morning beard and smiled at himself in the mirror. "Sounds intriguing. Only I'm not sure how solid you are out in the field. You're probably rusty. Will you be able to cover me if things go south?" he teased.

"Shut up. Don't forget, I'm not only a US Deputy Marshal but also a Marine Corps brat."

"How could I forget? I'll be standing tall, locked and cocked, in front of the general in a couple of weeks because of you."

Emory laughed. "So, how about it? Wanna haul Gryms's ass down to Denver with me? I thought we could take our time coming home. Make a road trip out of it."

"I don't know. I feel vulnerable with my boss suggesting I spend a few days with her alone on a work trip. Is this sexual harassment? Do we have an HR department?"

"You'll have to complain to Teresa, but I doubt she'll have your back now that she and I are friends."

"This sounds like a conspiracy allowing you to take blatant advantage of me."

"Busted." Emory's laugh warmed his heart. "How soon can you be ready to go?"

"I'll pack and pick you up in forty-five minutes."

Together, Dirk and Emory flew up to North Dakota. They accepted custody of Simeon Gryms and flew with him down to Denver. A pair of local deputy marshals took him to the courthouse from there.

After washing their hands of their charge, Dirk and

Emory checked in for the night at the Westin, a hotel built in the shape of wings on the south side of the main terminal building.

"Do you realize this is our first little 'get away' together?" Emory asked as she stood looking out the window at the planes taking off against a panoramic view of the Rocky Mountains.

Dirk circled his arms around her, bending to nuzzle her neck. "It was a great idea, boss. I'm ready for you to seduce me whenever you are."

36

———

The next day, they rented a car and drove north on I-25. Snow flurries grazed the windshield as they pulled into Cheyenne at dinnertime. Dirk took Emory to a local diner he knew.

"You'll like this place. It's a hole in the wall decorated in a western 50s motif, and their burgers are outstanding." When they sat, Dirk scanned the menu, but his mind wandered. "Hey, since we're driving through Wyoming, what do you think about meeting my friend Caitlin? We've been meaning to get together for months at the gun range in Sheridan for a shoot off. She's an excellent shot. Sometimes I win, but mostly she does. Want in?"

"Absolutely. Besides, I know you two are close. I'd love to meet her."

After they ordered dinner, Dirk called Caitlin to set up the shoot.

Luckily, Caitlin was available the next afternoon. "You really are a glutton for punishment, aren't you, Sterling?"

she laughed. "How are you going to feel when you get shut down by two women?"

"Never gonna happen." They made plans to meet at the range at three o'clock the following day.

In the end, after two hours of target practice, Emory owed Caitlin dinner, and Dirk had to buy them all a round from the bar. They went to Dirk and Caitlyn's usual after-shooting pub, whose only decorations were neon or antlers. When the beer showed up, Emory took the pints off the tray and passed them around.

She raised her glass. "Impressive shooting, Caitlyn. Anytime you want to come work in Montana, you just let me know. Where did you learn to handle a weapon like that?"

"I'm the youngest of three, with two older cowboy brothers. We grew up on a cattle ranch, and I had to keep up with them, I guess."

"Well, I was rustier than I thought." Emory grinned. "The hazards of riding the desk. Dirk," she grabbed his forearm, "promise me when you meet my dad on Thanksgiving, you will mention none of this."

Dirk tapped his glass against hers. "Not a chance, darlin'. Your father needs to know I'm a better shot than you and that I can protect you if I need to."

Caitlin took a long draw from her beer and, with a wicked gleam in her eye, said, "I guess, as the reigning shooting champion, *I'll* have to come to dinner to protect *you,* Dirk. You obviously know *nothing* about dads and their little girls." She clinked her glass against Emory's.

"Yeah, yeah. Whatever." He took a swig of his hoppy

brew. "Hey, Reed, I'm sorry your better half couldn't come with you. I haven't seen Colt in a long time."

"He was bummed he couldn't make it, but there are still only two of them working in the Sheriff's Office, and today was his deputy's day off."

Caitlin waved the server over to order dinner. Emory asked for tacos, and Dirk and Caitlyn ordered steak. Caitlyn gathered the menus and handed them to the waitress. "I heard you finally brought down Beaux Crandall. Solid work, Sterling. Impressive."

"Yes, it was." Emory agreed. Her appraisal embarrassed him and made him feel like a million bucks at the same time. "Dirk also uncovered the FBI mole who helped Crandall escape in the first place." Her voice rang with pride.

Brushing off the praise, Dirk changed the subject. "What's next for you, Reed?"

"Well, thanks to you, I have an interview with SOG."

Emory sat forward. "That's outstanding, Caitlyn. They're an elite unit. And from what I hear, you'd be a fantastic addition. Dirk says your dog is something to behold."

Caitlyn's grip tightened on her glass as she stared at its contents. "Renegade is the best dog there ever was."

"Sounds like it. Do you and Colt have kids?"

The light in Caitlyn's eyes died. "No." She hid behind several gulps of beer.

Dirk rushed in to change the subject. He should have warned Emory of the land mines. "I've got to tell you about Bear. You won't believe what he did when Caleb and Laurie were in danger." Dirk told Caitlyn the story of how Bear attacked Aldrich and broke his arm.

Caitlyn seemed to recover herself, and she smiled at the tale. "Aldrich is lucky Bear let go. He could have torn his arm clear off." She ate a few fries and then pointed one at Dirk. "You know, Laurie needs to find a life away from you hooligans. And I might know just the guy who can give it to her."

"Is that so?" Dirk rolled his eyes skyward. "Since when did you become a matchmaker?"

"Since right now."

"What Laurie needs is to be left alone for a while."

"Says her protector." Emory winked at Caitlyn. "Let me know if I can help."

After they finished their dinner, Emory excused herself to go to the restroom. Once she was out of earshot, Caitlin slugged Dirk's arm. "Well done, Sterling. Emory is amazing! But she is way too good for you."

"That's the understatement of the century. I don't know how I lucked out."

"So—you're meeting her parents, huh? That's a gargantuan step for you. Is there a future for the two of you?"

Dirk held her gaze for an extended moment before he bobbed his head. "For the first time in a long time, I think I might be ready to stick around."

DIRK AND EMORY stayed the night in Sheridan, even though it was only a two-hour drive back to Billings. They didn't want their time away together to end. They rented a room at a bed-and-breakfast cabin that had a four-poster bed and a fireplace.

They lay in under the blankets listening to the flames crackle and watching them cast dancing shadows around the room. "Next time we sneak away, we should spend a weekend up at my cabin." Dirk played with the strands of golden hair that were splayed across his chest.

"I'd love that. You have a beautiful place. If it were mine, I'd be up there every day I had off."

"Oh, yeah? Let's do it, then."

"Dirk?" Emory pressed herself up to look at him. "Where do you see yourself in five years?"

He smirked. "Is this a promotion interview? 'Cuz I like the job I have. My boss is very accommodating." Dirk leaned forward to kiss her and roll her to her back.

"I'm serious. I want to know."

"I don't know, Em." He trailed kisses along her jawline. "I'd like to think I'll be alive, working at my job, and still sleeping with you. Why?"

His mouth headed south, but Emory remained distracted. "Do you ever think you'll have kids?"

Goose bumps prickled all over his skin. Dirk clenched his jaw as the rest of his body stilled. He breathed in through his nose and flopped over on his back, staring at the ceiling while he tried to calm the calamity of emotions her question set off. "I'm going to put another log on the fire," he growled.

He rolled off the bed and tossed a chunk of wood on the flames, but he didn't get back in bed. Instead, he leaned against the mantel and watched the blue heat flicker on and off at the base of the fire.

"Hey," Emory called to him from the rumpled bed. "Did I say something wrong?"

"No."

"But... you don't want to answer?"

"No, Emory," His voice was sharp. "I don't want kids. Is that a good enough answer for you?"

She pulled the covers up over her bare skin and sat up against the headboard. The green in her eyes fractured in the fire light as she studied him. Her silence made him feel worse, so Dirk strode to the mini-fridge and snagged a beer. With his back to her, he stared out the window at the parking lot below while he drank it.

Returning to the heat, he sat on one of the two matching chairs on either side of the fireplace. Her gaze never left him.

"What?" he snapped.

"You tell me. Why are you angry?"

Dirk let loose a great sigh. "I'm not angry. I just don't want to talk about the next five years or kids or... anything."

"Okay."

She was so damn calm it drove him mad. "I suppose you're wondering all this because you like to fantasize about us getting married and having a bunch of kids, right? Do you not see what our job does to the people around us? It's bad for marriages *and for* families. I will not be responsible for wrecking lives."

Her gaze remained as level as her tone. "You're making a lot of assumptions."

"Am I wrong?"

"Not about everything. I know Laurie lost Sam and

that Henry and Amy are struggling, but Teresa would be a single mom no matter where she worked. And what about your friend Caitlyn and her husband? It sounds like they're happy."

"They don't have kids." A band tightened around his heart until the words finally escaped. "They were pregnant, a little while ago, but Caitlyn lost the baby in a car accident. One that would never have happened if she wasn't a law enforcement K9 handler."

Emory sprang from the bed as tears filled his eyes. She knelt at his feet and took his hands in hers. "That's why she shut down when I asked her about kids. I feel awful." She squeezed his fingers but softened her voice. "And I'm sorry for you too, because of your son."

A dagger pierced his soul, and the breath rushed from his lungs. His ears rang, and his pulse skyrocketed. He pulled his hands away and stared at her. He never talked about that. "How—?"

Emory bowed her head. "I read about it in your file."

Dirk stood and brushed by her, leaving her naked on the floor. He tossed a quilt at her. "Get dressed. I want to go home."

"Now? It's two in the morning. Can't we talk about this? I'm sorry I upset you."

"And I'm sorry you felt the need to pry into my private business."

"I read Henry and Teresa's files, too. It's my job to know my team and to be aware of anything that could be... a problem." Emory wrapped the quilt around her and walked toward him. "But either way, you told me you love me. And I love you, too. At the bare minimum, I think that means we want to be together, right?"

"At a bare minimum," he bit back with sarcasm. She was poking too close to his pain. Lashing out seemed the only way to keep her at bay. "Is this why your parents are coming? You're hoping for a big white wedding and a dozen kids?"

"No!" Finally, he'd goaded a spark of anger out of her. "But I want to share our lives with each other. That's not asking too much, is it? And at least I have bigger dreams than merely staying alive and sleeping together."

Emory yanked her suitcase from the closet and stuffed her legs into a pair of black leggings. She threw an oversized sweater on over that and started for the door.

"Where do you think you're going? It's snowing outside." His voice cracked.

She glared at him before jamming her feet into her boots and grabbing his coat. "I need some air." She opened the door and stalked into the hallway and down the stairs to the front entrance.

Dirk watched her from the window as she paced the parking lot without a hat or gloves. God—he'd royally screwed up. He'd overreacted, but why did Emory have to ruin what they had? Why couldn't things stay the same? They hadn't even been together for very long, and already she wanted more.

Finally, Emory slowed her gait and returned to the cabin. He heard her tread on the stairs and opened the door for her. She passed by him, shoving his icy coat against his bare chest. "I agree. We should leave. But not before we get a couple hours of sleep." She kicked off her snow-caked boots and got into bed, fully clothed, and scooted as far to the edge as possible before she yanked up the covers.

"Em..." His voice was thick with emotion and regret. "I'm sorry. You brought up things I never talk about. I wasn't prepared. That's all."

"It's fine."

"No, it's not. Nothing about it is fine. But you're right. I should be able to talk about it with you. How about we go up to my cabin next weekend? I'll tell you everything you want to know. Then you can decide if you still want me to meet your parents."

She rolled over to look at him then. The heat had dissipated from her eyes. "Why wouldn't I?"

"Because I can't give you the future you dream of." God knew Dirk loved Emory more than anything and that he wanted to spend his life with her. He couldn't ask Emory to give up on her dreams of a family. But there was no way he could risk having another child. Losing Bennett had nearly killed him. He wouldn't survive a loss like that again.

Emory rose from the bed and crossed the room. She lifted her hands and cupped his face forcing him to look at her. "Dirk, *you* are the future I want. The rest is negotiable."

To be continued...

THANK YOU FOR READING **REDEMPTION.** I hope you enjoyed chasing fugitives with Dirk Sterling through the mountains of Montana and beyond. The next book in the US Marshal Thriller Series continues Dirk's story and his fight for Justice, Integrity, and Service with the US Marshals Service.

Order WITSEC Now!

If you enjoyed reading REDEMPTION, Book 3 in the US Marshal Thriller Series, I would be most honored if you would please write a quick review.

Review REDEMPTION

Thank you!

***

Next!

Book 4 in the US Marshal Thriller Series

WITSEC

The Bennington's appear to be the all-American dream family until their daughter, Melissa, witnesses the chilling murder of her closest friends. Forced to flee from the ruthless killers, the entire family enters the federal witness protection program.

Assigned to safeguard the Bennington's in their new life in Billings, Dirk Sterling and his US Marshals team anticipate a routine assignment. However, their task takes a dangerous turn when a trio of assassins descends upon the town with one objective: to eliminate Melissa.

As the chaos unfolds, Dirk and his partner Hank find themselves confronting a daunting challenge. In the history of the Witness Protection Program, no witnesses who have followed the rules have ever been found. The question is, who broke the rules that led the killers to Billings. With bullets whizzing, Dirk and Hank must defy the odds to shield the family from a fate that could mark the program's first epic failure.

Order Your Copy Today!

~

For free books and to join my reader group,
Please visit my website.
Jodi-Burnett.com

ALSO BY JODI BURNETT

Run For The Hills

Hidden In The Hills

Danger In The Hills

A Flint River Christmas (Free Epilogue)

A Flint River Cookbook (Free Book)

FBI-K9 Thriller Series

Baxter K9 Hero (Free Prequel)

Avenging Adam

Body Count

Concealed Cargo

Mile High Mayhem

Tin Star K9 Series

RENEGADE

MAVERICK

CARNIVAL (Mid-Series Novella)

MARSHAL

JUSTICE

BLOODLINE

TRIFECTA

<u>QUALIFIED</u> (Mid-Series Novella)

<u>TRIALS</u>

<u>SPEC OPS K9</u>

US Marshal Dirk Sterling Trilogy

<u>FORGED</u> (<u>Free Prequel</u>)

<u>EXTRACTION</u>

<u>CORRUPTION</u>

<u>REDEMPTION</u>

ACKNOWLEDGMENTS

Thank you to my family and friends who supported me and encouraged me during the writing of REDEMPTION. As always, I'd like to thank my alpha and beta-readers and editors for scrutinizing my plot and helping to shape and polish my words.

Books are not solo ventures, and once the words are published, they need to be read and enjoyed for the work to be complete. So, thank you my dear readers for the finishing touches of my work. I truly couldn't do what I do without you.

Mostly, I want to thank God for the gift of imagination and the ability to paint it with words. Thank you to my husband, Chris, who suffers my artistic struggles with me and encourages me through them. Thanks for all the love and support, honey!

ABOUT THE AUTHOR

Jodi Burnett is a Colorado native and a mountain girl at heart. She loves writing Mystery and Suspense Thrillers from her mountain home in the Colorado Rockies where she dotes on her dogs and horses, complains about her cows, and writes to create a home for her imaginings. She is the author of both novels and novellas over four series: The Flint River Series, FBI K9 Thrillers, Tin Star K9, and the US Marshal Thrillers. Redemption is her seventeenth book. Jodi's books are available in paperback, eBook, and audiobook formats.

Connect with Jodi at Jodi-Burnett.com, on Facebook @ JodiBurnettAuthor, on Instagram @ JodiBurnettAuthor, or on Twitter @ Jodi_writes. Get free books by Burnett on her website.